Grand
View

Grand View

A Young Man's Trek to Love in Northern Minnesota

DAVID RALPH JOHNSON

This is a work of fiction. Names, characters, places, businesses, events, locales, and incidents are either the products of the author's imagination or used in a fictitious manner. Any resemblance to actual persons, living or dead, or actual events is purely coincidental.

DEDICATION

To Theresa and Russ: Your confidence in me brought these words to page.

Thank you.

Contents

Chapter 1 - Naked Winking Lady

"Another pot of hot. Jesus, Mary, and Joseph. Another pot of hot." These were mild words for Amile the chef that morning, meaning he was cranky and dry instead of his usual cranky and tuned.

Day before payday. He was out of money and therefore vodka. He hadn't metered things quite right the week past. Normally vodka had Amile hanging sheets of expletives on the line faster than the laundry ladies on Wednesdays.

In contrast, his words that day were almost pleasant. They were directed at me – the rookie Grand View Lodge dishwasher. I'd been on the job for two weeks. Dishwashing was a snap to master, and in the process, I'd learned most of the kitchen lingo.

For example, "pot of hot". A pot of hot required me to put three quarts of scalding water from the Bunn-o-Matic into a tall stainless-steel container. Then transmit the burning vessel to the cook line so Amile could resume his poached egg delicacies.

Pot of hot was a hazardous endeavor. The kitchen was a high-traffic area making navigation hairy. And a bump and a spill meant a burnt hand or wrist for me. Jesus, Mary, and Joseph indeed. I got the pot of hot to Amile without incident.

"Thanks Davie. Good boy."

"Any time, Amile," I replied. It felt good to be appreciated by Amile. He was rough and tumble, with a blue anchor tattoo on one forearm and a winking naked lady on the other. The lady's substantial breasts undulated when he flipped pancakes. He'd been around the world and knew what real work was. A thank you from Amile carried weight.

I returned to the dishwashing station and manned my post. Lodge guests were arriving in the dining room for their family breakfasts and it would be busy soon.

The guests were served by the Lodge dining room staff – kids of college age and college caliber. Each was smart, good looking, and well spoken. These were the traits that the Lodge owners sought when hiring. While well-behaved when on the clock, the college kids were quite the rowdy bunch on their free time. I felt a good summer looming in such company, one ripe with adventure.

I fired up the dishwasher and got to work on the first round of breakfast dishes.

Chapter 2 - Hired

I came up to Grand View Lodge with my best friend Rob and his girlfriend Annie. It was the summer of 1970. Rob had been job hunting that spring and came upon a want ad in the Minneapolis Star newspaper placed by Grand View Lodge seeking summer help.

Knowing I needed a summer job too, he gave me a call. "Dave, Grand View Lodge up in Nisswa is looking for help. It's on Gull Lake. Big resort area. Party time all summer long. Annie and I are going to check it out. Get out of Dodge for the summer. You interested?"

"Dodge" was our hometown of St. Anthony Village, a northeastern suburb located in the Twin Cities of Minneapolis and St. Paul. Working up north at a resort for one endless summer party sounded way better than riding the summer out flipping burgers at Sandy's Restaurant in the Village.

"Absolutely. Count me in Rob," I said.

My friends were the model *Teen Now* magazine couple. Rob had a handsome winning smile that accompanied a bodybuilder physique. Annie was a petite, classic Swede beauty, also physically fit. Whispers of teen envy trailed behind them when they walked the hallways of St. Anthony Village High.

Annie was the brains of the pair. Her A's went straight. Rob was the brawn of the pair. His A's were parked in Phy Ed. Both were avid athletes with Annie starring in gymnastics and Rob in downhill skiing.

I was an average Joe in looks and physical feats. My A's were sporadic. I was drawn to people who were outgoing, particularly ones walking a different path, like my buddy Rob. So, I readily jumped at Rob's Grand View Lodge prospect.

"OK, Dave. I'll call the number in the want ad and get us applications."

Rob made it happen. He set up personal job interviews for us with the Lodge general manager Fred Laszlo, Sr. at the Curtis Hotel in downtown Minneapolis. The Curtis and Grand View Lodge were owned by the same family and Fred operated out of the Curtis when hiring for Grand View. That made it convenient for us since downtown Minneapolis was a quick jaunt from the Village.

We got to the Curtis for our interviews early on a Saturday morning. Fred was situated there in a walnut paneled office behind a grand desk, wearing a tailored three-piece suite. His fingernails were trimmed and polished. That was a first for me. Money has a look.

We introduced ourselves. Fred smiled kindly and said, "Good morning. I'm Fred Laszlo. What brings you three here today?"

I was a bit intimidated by all the walnut and Fred's formality. My brain had no job-securing response at the ready. However, Rob forged right ahead with, "We want to work at Grand View Lodge this summer. What do you have for us, Fred?"

Fred smiled at that. He scanned a typed paper list in front of him. "Well Rob, Annie, and Dave, the Lodge has openings for a beach boy, a dining room waitress, and a dishwasher."

"Sounds good," said spokesman Rob. Annie and I nodded in agreement. I saw what was coming though. Given their good looks, Rob and Annie were the best choices for the guest-facing jobs. That left me with the pot-and-pan-facing job. But I really didn't mind. I wasn't expecting my Lodge job to groom me to be a brain surgeon. I would take what I could get to be there.

Fred drummed the paper list with his fingers while he contemplated what job offers to make. He looked us over for a final time, and said, "OK, how about Rob, beach boy; Annie, waitress; and Dave, dishwasher? Pay is the same for each job – $28 a week with room and board included, plus a bonus of $80 if you stay the whole summer." He clasped his perfect hands and closed with, "Grand View is not a big money venture for you. But I can promise you a summer of ad-venture. The people are great. And the food you'll eat is right from the chef's kitchen."

Fred sold us in a New York minute with those words – adventure was indeed what we were seeking. We all said, "OK," at the same time. He stood up, stretched over his desk, and cordially shook each of our hands to lock the deal.

We were headed for Grand View Lodge two weeks later.

Chapter 3 - Where One Slept

Upon arrival at Grand View, we were put up in old ramshackle staff cabins located on the very outskirts of the Lodge grounds.

The staff cabins were what remained of the original Lodge guest cabins, long since replaced by modern ones. They looked somewhat abandoned but were sound enough for summertime staff shelter.

Rob and I shared cabin "C" with three other guys. I had the porch room. Rob and the rest each had a cabin room.

A long hallway divided the cabin and ended at a communal bathroom, which was oddly colored all red. Having to pee bad on arrival, I saw it first.

"Hey Rob, check this out."

He dropped his gear in his room and came down the hall to see.

Toilet, toilet seat, sink, bathtub, floor, walls, and all were blood red. We would learn later that someone named "Turk" decided in a drunken moment to marry spare red paint from the shed outside to all surfaces from the bathroom door on. The bare bulb in the red porcelain socket over the sink still showed a few red flakes, the rest having burnt off since the paint job.

We laughed. Our adventure had begun.

Rob returned to his room as I peed and flushed via the red toilet handle.

I unpacked in the porch room. It was sparsely furnished. A single mattress on an iron spring frame occupied the north wall. The bed had a tilt that followed the slope of the porch floor. A bed stand with a windup Westclox alarm clock leaned accordingly.

A three-drawer dresser rounded out the picture, perfect for my limited wardrobe as I was no slave to fashion in those days, nor could I afford to be.

The porch room had walls of old six-light windows that hinged open to big panels of screen. Dense green forest lay beyond. Lying in bed at night was one degree from tent camping.

Rob's room matched mine for accoutrements. He would frequent his room when he wasn't sleeping over with Annie. That was driven by the frequency that Annie was alone in her cabin. In turn, that was driven by the frequency that Annie's roommate slept over with her boyfriend at his cabin.

Who slept where would be tightly connected to roommate vacancies "de la nuit."

Chapter 4 - Waitresses

Annie landed in cabin "A" with two other waitresses – Lisa and Maria. She was the young one of the bunch with the others being college age.

They satisfied Grand View requirements for looks and smarts. By coincidence, they were all the same height – five foot six inches. Size-wise, they could have been three paper dolls cut from the same paper stock. But each had their own look and personality.

Annie was athletic and outgoing. Lisa was dark and sultry, and a thinker. Maria was fair and willowy, and quiet, but she could rise to boisterous when the opportunity presented itself.

They were witty, enjoyed people, and a good fit for keeping Lodge guests in vacation mood. There was rarely a lull in conversation around their cabin. They let no one, such as me, be shy for very long. I liked them all for the natural ease I felt in their company.

Their cabin was most pleasant. While Rob and my cabin looked and smelled seriously sparse and male inhabited, theirs was decorated nicely and had an enticing aroma, the scent of fresh laundry. The scent was not intentional, but the result of a southerly breeze that wafted past the Lodge laundry and into their cabin windows most days. Such pretty girls, enveloped in the scent of fresh laundry, struck a chord in me that I named desire. That desire would take me past their place, even when I wasn't going past their place.

I fell for Lisa right off the bat. She was exotic, being from a distant land – Boston. It was distant to me anyway. My relationships so far in life had been limited to a triangle of family and friends with Minnesota vertices of Hutchinson, Paynesville, and the Twin Cities.

Lisa's first words to me were, "Please hold the door open." She was moving her stuff into the cabin on the day we met. Her Boston accent went into my head and swirled around and triggered my heart to race and other things to take rise. Urgent flammable things. I held the door very open and said, "There you go."

Desire, coupled with urgent flammables, struck a chord in me that I named infatuation.

My infatuation with Lisa would take us along an interesting path soon that summer.

Chapter 5 - The Beach

Grand View Lodge had three hundred feet of beach on Gull Lake in northern Minnesota. Perfect blond sand graced its shoreline. The Lodge beach hut was situated on the north end of the beach. It had a traditional tiki hut design, complete with a pointed palm thatch roof. Protruding from the right side was a modern rectangular building that housed the Lodge pool and sauna.

The beach was managed by Dave C. and his assistant Turk. The two of them ran the fishing boat rental, took Lodge guests out waterskiing, and kept all the beach activities supported.

As the Lodge beach boy, Rob got his work orders from them both. Rob was low man on the tiki hut totem pole and did most of the grunt work to keep the perfect beach perfect. Doing so required combing the beach sand to a pristine condition each morning. Occasionally he'd have to roust a guest awake who was sleeping off a drunk on the beach from the night before, and get the guest moving toward hangover time. As a final touch, Rob would align the white beach chairs with their blue umbrellas, so the beach area matched exactly that shown on postcards in the Lodge gift shop.

All three guys partnered throughout the day to dole out candy bars, pop, and chips to the kids at the snack bar, repair beach equipment when needed, and keep the pool running and the sauna steaming.

Boat motors were maintained by Turk in the Lodge boat shed nearby. The shed was an original Lodge shelter, circa 1929. It was dank and smelled of boat motor oil and old gasoline. Fishing rods, life vests, anchors, and such were neatly organized on the walls and floor. For those with time to kill, the shed was the place to yak with Turk while he puttered on motors. Talk included the latest skinny on Lodge girls, fishing, fast cars, boat motor mechanics, sports, and of course Lodge girls.

In our first encounter with Turk, he looked Rob and me up and down and asked, "What cabin are you two homos sharing?" Turk liked to start a conversation with startling words.

Rob and I traded wondering glances. Rob said, "Cabin C. And we're not homos."

"Well the summer's still young," Turk replied. "Hey, how do you like the red bathroom? That's my doing."

"Very nice," I said.

"OK, girls. Glad to have you on board. I have to see a man about a horse," and he turned abruptly and set off in the direction of the beach Men's room to presumably relieve himself.

The "OK girls" meant we were in as shed members.

Dave C. and Turk augmented their Lodge wages with a sideline business selling used boat motors. Dave C. had a fast boat. A stripped down Glastron. A shell of a boat really. Fiberglass hull with an eighty-horse motor hanging off the stern. That was about it, and it went like hell. Boat motors for their business were procured during midnight runs on the lake. Dave C. and Turk would speed to their mark — some boat spotted previously with a nice motor facing lakeside. Lights out, they'd cut power and paddle in, steal the motor, then tear back to the Lodge, all horses engaged. The stolen motor would hang on a motor stand in the Lodge boat shed until they ran it down to the Cities for a quick sale.

I had never rubbed shoulders with bona fide thieves before. It was exciting, in a wrong kind of way of course. They were two mild-mannered mavericks with steel balls, lucrative midnight runs, and ill-gotten gains. Temptation to join them lurked in my head. I decided it was best to live their feats vicariously, given the Ten Commandments and potential jail time. Still, it was fun to imagine being an outlaw with money to burn and that glint in your eye that said you were outside the norm and you knew it and liked it. Dave C. had the glint.

Turk was tall, rotund, and strong beyond appearance. This was necessary for pulling boat motors from their mounts. Dave C., on the other hand, was lean and average in height, but with a sinewy strength that you didn't want to mess with. To boot, he had an endearing half-cocked smile fixed on his handsome boyish face most of the time. He was a lady killer but flew solo that summer. He had a girl back in the Cities that he was devoted to. But he traveled a one-way street in that relationship. He was madly in love with her, but she not so with him. Obsession was hard run, especially on empty.

Chapter 6 - GTO

The Mobile boys were the Lodge dining room bus staff that summer. Denny, Scott, and Terry set up and cleared the tables during the guest meals, which was two shifts a day, for breakfast and supper.

The three of them rounded out the group that I came to know so well that summer. They came up from Mobile, Alabama, in a new convertible GTO which was the prettiest car I'd ever seen. It was a graduation gift to Denny from his rich dad for completing high school. Denny's dad must have had deep pockets because this was a true muscle car, with high performance upgrades and flawless custom paint done professionally. The car pinned you back hard in its red tuck and roll when Denny put the pedal to the metal.

This crew from the Deep South taught me that I spoke with an accent. On the first night we partied together I mentioned that I liked their accent. They laughed at that and said, "Boy, y'all have the accent." Then they mimicked me, bantering back and forth using my precise Midwestern words. Their rendition of my speech sounded hilarious. Yet it was true. When I put my feet in their shoes, I realized I had an accent too. Somehow my world got a little bigger that night.

Regarding partying, the Mobile boys' cabin was a hot spot that summer. It was buried in the woods, far from any Lodge activity. And Denny had a fake Alabama driver license that put him on the legal side of Minnesota alcohol procurement.

Remote location, booze readily available at a reasonable markup, young adults, or almost young adults, in determined pursuit of adult things – these stars of debauchery aligned every payday Friday, or occasionally in between, and the party torch was lit.

The yellow bug light outside the Mobile boys' front door served as the party torch. Denny would throw it on around nine o'clock on nights they were open for partying.

My friend Rob and I were the almost young adults who frequented the Mobile boys' den of iniquity. A bottle of Boone's Farm apple wine could be had for a dollar. That included Denny's twenty-five cent markup, which made for an affordable evening buzz.

If we were up for high-test Ethyl, we'd pool our funds for a pint of vodka from Denny's stock. That we'd nurse until the early hours of the next day. Fueled with eighty proof enthusiasm, we'd argue the shortcomings of our world, resting on the cabin lawn under a night sky choked with stars.

They were such lovely arguments that summer, with solutions so naive, so at hand. With no real responsibility on our backs yet, we danced light on our intelligent toes.

Chapter 7 - Three Legs to Stand On

The Lodge dog was a mostly chocolate lab named Gertie. She had a white diamond on her chest, origin unknown, which made her a mix of some type.

Fred Laszlo hired her as Lodge dog ten years ago. She applied for the post by hanging around the Lodge beach hut persistently for days, looking half-starved but very happy to be with newfound friends. She had no collar so there was no way to trace her back to her owner.

Fred was a softy when it came to any person or animal in need. He decided the Lodge could use just such a nice dog. His family took her in, naming her Gertie and giving her the official position of Lodge dog.

Gertie was three-legged, having lost her right front a few summers ago chasing a car out on the two-lane that ran by the Lodge. She still chased cars, but she was reduced to half speed given her one tire was blown. Watching Gertie run was a bit mystical. She defied physics. One front leg kept up with two powerful ones behind, moving ears, body, and tail flying along. Her lost leg appeared invisibly still at work. How could that have been? But so it was. Most evenings Gertie hung out around the Lodge beach hut. Guests coming and going would stop for a chat and pet her. They were missing their own pets and she enjoyed filling the gap.

My summer with Gertie got off to a rollicking start. I was at the beach killing some time before my evening shift began. Gertie came up and plopped down at my feet. I gave her a few introductory rubs. We took to each other nicely, so I sat down too for a few more pets. I decided to bounce a few jokes off her.

I asked her, "How do you get a one-armed man out of a tree?"

She rotated her head a quarter turn with a puzzled look, as dogs do when curiosity strikes.

I answered, "You wave at him."

Gertie smiled at the punchline half-heartedly. I was expecting more dogged appreciation, as this was one of my better jokes. It dawned on me that I might have offended her, given her missing limb situation. I forged ahead figuring I would redeem myself with the second joke in my repertoire.

Gertie's attention suddenly changed. In an instant, she was up on her three paws, alert to something extraordinary.

Chunks of prime rib were falling from heaven.

It happened to be the first Beach Buffet Wednesday of the summer. The beach buffet truck was swinging by to deliver prime rib and fixings to waiting beach buffet guests.

Alonzo, chief cook's helper, was at the wheel. He'd forgotten to latch the side doors that kept the food in place in the rear box of the truck.

Alonzo was pushing eighty. He was a short little arthritic man, the product of many years as the human cannonball at Paul Bunyan Land amusement park nearby. He had a nip of booze every afternoon to keep his arthritis in check. Just before loading the truck that afternoon, he'd tripled his medication due to a chill. That caused more than his normal absent mindedness, which led to the missed door latches.

With a good buzz on, food doors flapping wildly, Alonzo rounded the beach hut corner with purpose.

Inertia took hold and prime rib flew out the doors.

Gertie was near speech when she got to the flying meat spectacle. She scored two pieces of prime before Dave C. and Turk chased her off.

Seeing the prime rib pass by in Gertie's jowls and her at full three-legged throttle, Alonzo realized a spill must have occurred. He hit the brakes and backed up.

Being out of sight from the guests, Alonzo and Dave C. and Turk decided the spill was salvageable with some good wiping off. I helped, and everything was restored in a few minutes. Alonzo proceeded to his delivery.

The beach buffet guests mentioned no issues with the prime rib that night.

Gertie thought the same, resting, belly full, a few hundred feet down the beach.

"It was medium rare. Just right," Gertie said to me about the event the next time we met. I smiled a big smile, with dogged appreciation, and proceeded with my first joke of the evening.

Chapter 8 - Lisa

I had named it infatuation, but my feelings for Lisa were more than a single word. They were a poem that made a morning of dishwashing effortless, watching her figure come and go as she carried her orders in and out the dining room doors.

I rode that poem for weeks, but to no avail. Lisa was aloof when I had any chance to interact with her. She would smile nicely when our eyes happened to meet, but that was it. Barely a word was exchanged between us other than brief pleasantries.

By chance I found out why she was a bit distant. Between my dishwashing shifts one hot afternoon, I was walking the path up to the Mobile boys' cabin to see what they would have in stock for refreshments later. That took me directly by Lisa's.

As I neared, a rise in the path provided a view of Lisa's window, open with lace white curtains drifting lazily to and fro. There I caught a glimpse of two girls standing inside, kissing in a passionate embrace and naked from the waist up. Lisa and Maria. I had to think about that for a minute. Girls in a passionate embrace. My knowledge in that realm was the word naive. The life I knew held people with relationships on the straight and narrow. Two girls getting it on was a new one to me.

I walked on.

Funny how life throws things at you. You can have a thousand glimpses on any day that go unregistered, but then one comes along that locks itself to your brain and throws away the key. The image of Lisa and Maria locked in under "E" for erotic. Unfortunately, in the "L" for love department, their caress pretty much smoked my chances with Lisa. Bummer.

I arrived soon after at the Mobile boys' cabin. The place was empty, and the GTO was gone, so I assumed the boys were making a refreshment run.

I turned west and took the long way home via the lakeshore path. I revisited things newly filed in my memory banks under "E". The topic got me to my cabin in no time, with a burn to put new definition on sweet release. I did so in two minutes, with fervor, then spun out of my room headed for my next shift on a wave of afterglow.

That night, I smiled at Lisa as she swung through the dining room doors with her first order. She smiled back and gave me a wink. Perhaps she'd seen me too on my walk that day. That possibility I named intrigue. The summer was certainly getting interesting.

Chapter 9 - Mission

Turk was leaning over the candy counter in the Lodge beach hut, beating an Old Gold.

He tapped its ashes carelessly on the floor with a flick of his index finger. He didn't have much regard for cleanliness. Or rules.

He was contemplating the sun setting. The candy counter offered the perfect view through its west facing picture window. The big orange ball was touching the horizon. The sky was taking the hint for twilight.

I came in with the screen door slamming behind me, nearly tripping on Gertie. I normally knew to sidestep her usual post, but I was moving fast and forgot. As I recovered to upright, Turk asked, "Hey Davie, how's the anal pore coitus these days?" Not knowing exactly what those words meant in that particular order, I ventured a "not bad." He smiled and took a drag off his cig, then said, "Good Davie, keep it up." His words came out in syllables of Old Gold smoke.

I really didn't have time for small talk. I was on a mission and needed to know where Dave C. was.

"Where's Dave C.?"

"Where's my five dollars?" More Old Gold syllables.

"C'mon Turk, do you know where Dave C. is?"

"So, you heard about the midnight run?"

I had. Rob said Dave C. was going to cross the lake that night for a visit to Madden's resort.

Madden's was a sprawling affair on the opposite side of the lake with plenty of dockside access. Full of wealthy boaters that liked to party all night. While Grand View was mostly quiet and for the family, Madden's was hell bent on fun.

"Yes. I'd like to go."

"I myself heard Dave C.'s got a full crew lined up. Maybe next time, Davie."

A full crew meant Dave C. and four others packed into his boat's stripped-down hull, bringing the water line up to the barely afloat level. So, no room for me that night.

"OK, Turk. Gotta get back for the evening shift. See ya."

"Keep on truckin' Davie."

I left for the kitchen and Turk returned to his sunset.

Chapter 10 - Midnight Run

Dave C. had the Glastron at the dock right after the night shift, ready for boarding. Its outboard motor was at a slow idle with exhaust exiting the propeller in bubbles of white smoke. The exhaust fumes added a lethal fragrance to the still night air.

Turk and the Mobile boys arrived as scheduled. They hopped in. Dave C. gunned the throttle and they were off.

The moon was full. The lake was smooth as black mirror. The Glastron cut a perfect moonlit wedge as it proceeded out. The boat's red and green navigation light on the bow led the way.

Dave C. had explained to me in one of our Lodge boat shed talks that the red light was on the left to indicate a boat's port side, and the green was on the right to indicate the starboard side. When two boats were coming at each other head on in the night, you kept green to green for safe passing.

And if the boats were on a collision course, the boat that sees the red nav light of the other must yield. Conversely, the other will see green, giving it the stand on position, meaning OK for it to stay on course.

Two simple colored lights kept it all straight.

There were no other nav lights to be seen on the vast expanse of water. The guys had Gull Lake to themselves.

They were making time. Dave C. had the throttle pushed forward all the way, and the motor roared the boat along at top end. Dave C. had the only seat. The others sat on life preserver cushions on the bottom of the boat. Its low-slung hull allowed all to see easily out.

Turk's cigarette was finished in half the time, with the wind taking the better part of it, sparks flying.

They had to take a dogleg to the right. If they had gone straight across the lake they would have gone over a rock pile that was submerged a foot under water, right in the middle of things. Fieldstone sized rocks were dumped there when a glacier receded from the area ten thousand years ago. The rocks were beautiful ancient things that also dotted lakeside retaining walls and cabin fireplaces.

Dave C. and crew arrived and tied off at a lone dock in Madden's marina. They were refreshed from the blast of night air their cruise had provided. Strands of clear bulbs illuminated the grounds in gentle swoops. A thousand yellow filaments dotted the air like fireflies lighting their way. Madden's convention center was their destination. It was glowing with activity. Music blared from within, and the base beat could be felt as they neared.

Chapter 11 - Home of the Huskies

Except for Denny, everyone else was underage according to their IDs.

Dave C. and Turk were a few months from twenty-one. Scott and Terry were nineteen. Technically, that kept the four of them out of Madden's drinking establishments. However, walking through and seeing if anyone took notice didn't require an ID.

Their first stop was the Kon Tiki Torch Room.

Torches with gas flames lit the walkway to the entrance. And torch shaped sconces angled out from the walls inside giving the room an amber glow. The image of Thor Heyerdahl coursing the Pacific on his Kon Tiki raft occupied the wall behind the bar. There were no loose ends in that room of torches. The only thing missing was a bouncer at the door. That got them inside, no sweat. The place was packed so they stood and took everything in. Terry caught the eye of a young woman. Not one for wasting the moment, he sauntered over and introduced himself.

"Hello, I'm Terry."

She replied, "Hello Terry, I'm Wendy."

Wendy looked him straight in the eyes. Eyes are meant to be looked into sincerely. They walk you directly to the edge of the cliff. Terry stood on the brink and looked straight into Wendy's.

Wendy asked, "And what brings you here, Mr. Terry?"

He replied, "Usually a fast boat, like one tonight." Mr. Smooth. "I'm up here this summer from Mobile, Alabama. I work across the lake at Grand View Lodge in the dining room."

"Well," Wendy smiled, "maybe you've seen me. I'm staying there with my mom and dad. They're around here somewhere with their friends from Minnesota."

Terry wondered at that. Road trip with mom and dad. That put Wendy younger than she looked. Seventeen maybe, although she passed for twenty-one, torch lit as she was.

"And where are you from Miss Wendy?" Terry asked.

"Minot, North Dakota. Home of the Huskies," she replied.

Yup. Seventeen.

Terry noticed Dave C. giving him a helicopter motion with his right index finger. The boys wanted to roam on. Takeoff time.

Terry had to stay with the boys or risk being left to hitchhike twelve miles home on the dark two-lane road around the lake. Getting back that way, before first shift started the next day, was fifty-fifty.

"Well Miss Wendy, my friends are about to go. So, I gotta go too. I hope to see you again." He so did.

"It was nice to meet you, Mr. Terry. I'll keep my eye out for you too."

They left the edge of the cliff and parted ways. Terry liked his new nickname, Mr. Terry, and the lovely girl that voiced it. Wendy liked their encounter as well.

Chapter 12 - Cutty Sark

Reunited, Dave C. and Turk and the Mobile boys cut through Madden's convention center bound for more action. Terry smiled to himself at the thought of seeing Wendy at breakfast tomorrow.

They approached an empty banquet room. Its double doorway revealed an expanse of forty round tables covered with white cloth and fancy wedding doodads. The doodads were in various stages of disarray after a night of wedding guest fiddling. One could judge that the room started off in spectacular fashion given all the colorful remnants lying about.

Madden's cleanup crew was cleaning tables in the back of the room, making progress toward the front.

A portable bar sat unattended by the head wedding table. Dave C.'s eye for things unattended caught the opportunity.

He ducked through the banquet doorway and grabbed a quart of unopened Cutty Sark scotch whisky. His exit was clean.

He merged with his companions who provided cover for the whisky transport like they'd been planning the heist all day long. They moved as one, knowing the mission, anticipating the taste, and feeling the rush. The score was good reason to head back to the boat

Once outside, they were free. A new bond had formed. Joint thievery. Fate's doing. They shared slight smiles as they moved on.

The night air had cooled. Under the light of the moon and swags of string lights, the boys retraced the path to the Glastron. It floated patiently, reined to the dock and ready.

They hopped back in, taking same spots as the trip there. Dave C. wrapped the Cutty Sark in a beach towel and tucked it under his seat for safekeeping. He fired up the motor as Turk undid their mooring. Away they went, slowly, then full throttle once they cleared the marina.

A few minutes out, Dave C. throttled down and idled the motor. He brought out the whisky, so the boys could have a round of sips. He twisted the bottle top, breaking the liquor seal with a crisp snap. Turk took the first swig. The whisky burned down his throat, but the afterglow was most pleasant. Same for the rest of the boys. Their spirits rose, those pirates of Gull Lake. When the bottle got to Dave C. he refrained. He had yet to drink in front of anyone at Grand View that summer, not at all really.

His use of alcohol had been tempered by his parents, both mean drunks. He liked to be in control of himself always; he did not want to chance being a fool like his folks.

Plus, being responsible for his friends meant staying sober.

The bottle made a second round, then was stowed for takeoff. Dave C. hit the throttle hard and got up to going like hell speed, just as a large cabin cruiser cut them off.

Chapter 13 - Rock Pile

The cabin cruiser came fast out of the night from the left. According to the cabin cruiser nav lights, Dave C. had the stand on position, the right of way. But whoever was at the cabin cruiser wheel forged straight ahead across the Glastron path, unaware of the smaller boat torpedoing toward it. Dave C. immediately took a hard right, sending the boys smashing into each other. He then straightened out, which caused them all to smash into each other the opposite way. The boys started to right themselves. Dave C.'s quick moves had saved their lives. But in the process, he had put them on course for another disaster, realized an instant later when the edge of the rock pile took the Glastron motor off. A good part of the boat's stern went with it. Dave C. lost all control at that point as the wheel went slack in his hands. They had been doing forty-five knots. They still had great momentum. When the stern tore loose the bow dipped, catching the rock pile and bouncing what was left of the hull airborne.

The boys flew out helter-skelter. Dave C. stayed put deep in his seat from G force. On final impact, spray flew forty yards as the hull cracked open, then sank without pause. The boys landed past the rock pile in eight feet of water. They hit the water hard as if they'd had a bad fall waterskiing at high speed. Denny surfaced first, followed by

Scott, then Turk. No Terry. Dave C. rode out the crash, letting the boat take the beating. Instinct kicked in, keeping him gripped white-knuckled to the boat wheel. He lucked out as the hull settled on the lake bottom with him setting upright. He was extremely shaken but aware enough to simply float to the surface.

They all made it back to the rock pile and crawled on to it. Still no Terry. Any attempt to stand was thwarted by slippery rock, so they sat instead in the shallow water that covered the rock pile. The water felt warmer than the night air. That would have been pleasant in other circumstances.

"What the fuck?" said Turk. "Where's Terry?"

They didn't know where or how to start looking. No one was thinking clearly. Shock and fear were taking over. The full moon had set making it too dark to see. They were engulfed in blackness.

Chapter 14 - Breakfast

A very lovely girl walked into the Lodge dining room the next morning. My age, I thought. She gave me a nice look.

I was too preoccupied to pay much attention. I was mastering the art of setting tables and would soon be bussing them. I'd had ten minutes of instruction from Lisa. On the job training. More like on the fly training.

The Mobile boys hadn't shown up for work that morning. No one knew why. They had never missed a shift before, so something was amiss.

Rob was hanging around Annie who was about to go on shift. Fred Laszlo commandeered him to go up to the Mobile boys' cabin and see what was up.

Off he went, and Fred gave me the call to bus in their place. That included a fresh white shirt, a black clip-on bow tie, and Lisa as mentor, which I didn't mind at all.

The wait staff and I would be doing double duty that morning.

Alonzo was covering the dishwashing as best his old body could.

The guests rolled in, and we were off to the races.

My goodness, that girl was pretty. I caught her glancing at me more than once. That meant she caught me glancing at her equally so. We tied in the glance department that morning. Her folks and she were casually dressed.

Nicely so. Welcoming, not stuffy like some of the rich guests. They took their time eating and chatting, perhaps about the coming day, and then left for it. She cleaned her plate. So I found when I cleared their table. Funny the attention to detail you pay when love at first sight is lurking about.

Other than a pair of stragglers, the dining room was empty an hour later. I caught up on bussing, then relieved Alonzo. He'd given it his best shot, but there was still a mountain of breakfast dishes to tackle.

"Hey Davie, I need to take five."

"OK, old man," I replied. "I'll take it from here."

He smiled gratefully, old weathered kind man that he was, and walked his bent body out the kitchen back door for a smoke, screen door slamming behind him.

I took the handoff and wrapped things up, only a half hour beyond my normal shift.

Chapter 15 - Rescue

Terry had been alive through the night, floating south of the boys, unable to communicate. He was riding backmost in the Glastron when its motor hit the rocks. The motor's powerhead surged forward and cracked Terry's collarbone. His position at the very back of the boat put him on the long end of a catapult when the boat bottomed out at forty-five knots. That flung him beyond the boys by thirty yards. Terry broke a rib when he slammed down on the water, seriously compounding his injury. His life cushion was in flight right behind him. It hit him square in the face. He grabbed it with his good arm and put its strap over his head and under his armpit. That kept him afloat.

The cracked collarbone and broken rib were both on his left side. That made pain so excruciating he could barely speak. His faint whispers for help were out of earshot of the boys on the rock pile. However, he could hear them plain as day. Terry was touched when they repeatedly called for him, when he heard their anguish at the thought of him gone. And later when they spoke of what a good guy he was. Their words made him evermore determined to ride out the pain and get his ass saved. But he could barely move, so he had to float where he was and play bobber for the duration.

As dawn approached, Terry and the boys finally caught sight of each other.

Denny was first to spot him. He couldn't believe his eyes. He exclaimed, "Terry! God damn, Terry! There he is! There he is!"

Dave C. jumped in and swam out and towed Terry back, lifeguard style, to the rock pile.

Terry was in agony as he was pulled up on the rocks, but cracked a half smile at the boys, who were beyond jubilant to have him alive in their midst.

Dave C. said, "OK we're good now. Won't be long before someone out fishing sees us and comes to the rescue."

Turk piped in, "What a night. What a fucking night. This was one for the books. Good to be fucking alive."

They all fucking agreed, as the first boat of the morning came from the north to their rescue.

Chapter 16 - Facts and Drama

Rob was looking for me after I left the kitchen that morning. I was wandering the Lodge grounds deciding what to do until the evening shift. Our paths crossed at the Lodge tennis court.

Two tennis newbies had been sending tennis balls over the court fence with some regularity, based on the number of balls scattered about the lawn. Their bucket of balls was better than half gone. They were switching sides, so we stopped, said, "Hello guys," and tossed the errant balls back one by one. They waved their racquets in appreciation.

As they resumed their game of mostly sending tennis balls over the court fence, Rob led off with big news, "Dave, everybody on the midnight run last night is missing. Dave C.'s boat is gone too. Fred Laszlo is at the beach hut right now on the phone to the sheriff's office."

I looked at Rob. His expression was hard to read, but excited. This was serious. Five friends were in deep trouble, or worse, dead.

For the first time in either of our lives, we were involved in a real potential tragic situation. We were feeling a jumble of emotions.

In any tragedy there is cold fact, and there is emotional drama. You choose from these two in your response. Fact takes you somewhere tangible. Drama gets you there with speed. Without both, you churn.

We had minimal facts to go on. Drama took over.

"Jesus," I said. "I was almost on Dave C.'s boat last night. Turk waved me off."

"Turk did the same to me too," Rob replied. "That could've been us out there. Man, I hope they're OK."

"Me too. What now?" I asked.

"Well, we stick around and wait for some word, I guess," Rob said.

That word was not too far off, as Dave C. and the boys were crossing the lake in an overloaded fishing boat, heading for the Lodge dock.

Chapter 17 - The Landing

Fred Laszlo was at the beach hut and saw the boys coming in from the lake, just as his call was connected to Deputy Sheriff Thomas.

Fred said, "Hang on Sheriff. The reason I am calling is just floating up to my dock."

Without waiting for a response, Fred put the phone receiver down hard on the candy counter and headed out the screen door for the dock. Deputy Sheriff Thomas heard the bangs of the receiver and the screen door and figured he was on hold. He went back to his morning toast and coffee.

Fred got to the dock as the boys arrived. They were crowded into their rescue craft, a tiny Alumacraft fishing boat. The man at the tiller killed the motor and glided the boat to a soft landing.

Fred tied the boat off to a dock piling. He could see that Terry was in rough shape.

Dave C. said, "Fred, we had a near miss last night with another boat that drove us into the rock pile. Terry's hurt pretty bad."

Fred took charge. "OK, Terry out first. Explanations later. Can you make it up on your own, Terry?"

Terry nodded yes.

"Dave C. and Turk, help him up and steady him," Fred instructed. "Denny, get up on the dock and help Terry when he gets there."

They did so. It was a high step up from the boat. Dave C. and Turk hoisted from behind, and Denny gently brought Terry to an upright position on the dock.

Fred said, "OK. We'll take the Caddy. Next stop the Brainerd hospital emergency room. Who besides Terry needs to see a doctor? Don't worry about cost. I have it covered."

Remarkably, everyone else was in pretty good condition. They were cold and wet and bruised from six hours on the rock pile, but they had youth and stamina on their side which gave their bodies and souls the means to bounce back quickly. The morning sun was warming their bones. That helped. And their spirits were riding high from surviving near death which was no exaggeration.

Dave C. assessed the condition of his pirate crew and said, "We're good, Fred." They all nodded in agreement. Dave C. continued, "I'll go with you to the ER and help out with Terry. Terry, that OK with you?"

"It is. Thanks Dave C. It is," Terry whispered.

"You there," Fred said to their rescuer, "stay put. Denny, go up to the Lodge lobby and get a free beach buffet dinner certificate for this man and his family."

Denny took off for the Lodge.

Dave C. supported Terry by his good arm and they walked in step to Fred's long black Cadillac. Terry laid down in the back seat which was ample enough for him to stretch almost completely out. He found a position on his right side that minimized the pain on his left, moaning as he settled in for the trip.

Fred and Dave C. got in the front seat. Fred liked any opportunity for a fast Caddy takeoff. The hospital run presented just such a moment. He started up the Caddy and launched it up the dirt lane bound for their Brainerd destination. His departure left everyone in a wide-track Cadillac cloud of dust.

Chapter 18 - Tree Swing

After our tennis court conversation, Rob and I split up. Rob headed to Annie's cabin to fill in the girls on the missing boys. I chose to wander the Lodge grounds some more. I saw a big black Cadillac fly past in the distance. Fred Laszlo would have objected to that. Guests were to obey the 10 mph speed limit signs posted all over.

As I approached the Lodge, I saw the pretty girl from breakfast that morning. She was sitting in the tree swing that hung from a great elm on the front lawn of the Lodge entrance. From her venue, two strands of rope ran parallel and disappeared up in the elm's leafy canopy. Sunlight filtered down through surrounding high pines and landed softly on the subtle pastels she wore. She sat ankles crossed, intent on something in her lap. Her long dark hair was draped over one shoulder. Renoir couldn't have painted a more fetching scene.

The Lodge behind her was built in the Roaring Twenties. It was a gargantuan structure, two stories high in the front and three in the back, made from native white pine logs that averaged two feet in diameter.

The original Lodge owners made a fortune in bootlegging back then, and they put a big share of it into the Lodge. When finished it was called the Jewel of the North.

A jewel it was still, as it made such a romantic setting for a lovely girl on a swing with a boy approaching.

As I walked near, I saw that she was writing in a book. It was one of those books with a hard cover filled entirely with blank pages. She was using a fountain pen. Since this was proper writing equipment, I was impressed.

She rested her pen as her eyes left the page. Her expression was one of satisfaction, as if her current thought or observation had landed just right in the words she had just written. Our eyes met, and her expression turned to interest.

Lodge staff were not to fraternize with Lodge guests. That was a big rule. Me fraternizing with her, in view of the entire Lodge, was risky. But I figured a simple Minnesota hello would be safe.

"Hello," I said.

"Hello," she replied.

"Are you writing a poem?" I fraternized.

"No, I'm writing in my journal," she replied.

She looked me straight in the eyes. I looked straight back. I felt that I was teetering on the edge of a cliff for some strange reason.

I couldn't leave now. I had to know more about this journal writing girl perched on a rope swing who cleaned her plate every morning.

I leaned casually on the tree with one hand like I had nowhere to be. The old twisted elm put a respectful fifteen feet between us.

"Well this is certainly a good place for writing," I said. "I write too." At that point I threw caution to the wind, crossing from fraternizing smack into tall-tale telling. Pursuit of love is such a slippery slope.

"That's good. I don't know too many people that write where I come from. Boys are jocks, mostly," she said. "And my girlfriends aren't into it. My real passion though is painting. Watercolors."

"My writing is just bits and pieces. Feels good to see it on paper," I said. Well that much was true. I did like to do that.

"Well, nice talking to you. I'm sorry I have to go," she said. "I'm already late to the beach for a swim with my family. What's your name, writer man?"

I fell off the precipice.

"Dave. And you, painter lady?"

"Wendy. See you again maybe?"

She had fallen too.

"Yes, Wendy. I'll look for you here same time tomorrow."

"Please do," she replied.

And so, we parted ways for twenty-four hours.

Chapter 19 - Rescue Recount

Terry would be overnight in the Brainerd hospital recovering from the boat crash. All the other pirates went back to working their normal shifts after the morning rescue.

Lodge staff were abuzz all day with the story of their tragedy on the water. After work that night we crowded into the Mobile boys' cabin for the recount.

Caught up in the moment, Denny passed out beers to everyone on the house. The beer was cold, making the bottles sweat with condensation from the humid night air. In party cabin ritual, a bottle opener was passed from one to another, and spent bottle caps were tossed neatly into the bottle cap box in the corner. After the last cap was stowed, the tribal gathering began.

Scott, the quiet member of the Mobile crew, led things off. He was the most animated I'd ever seen him.

Scott's enthusiasm was a new thing. He was normally a very slow talker, the result of being struck by lightning as a child.

When he was ten years old a lightning bolt hit the home chimney and sent a fireball into the kitchen below. The fireball floated slowly across the room, then fried the family's Frigidaire in a blue blinding flash. Scott wasn't hit directly but was sitting near enough to the fridge for the charge to blow his shoes off.

He was silent for six months after that. Doctors didn't know if his silence was a physical or emotional ailment. He eventually started talking on his own, but from then on only with the slow cadence we knew him by.

That night after the crash however, he was talking a mile-a-minute. Perhaps some brain wiring got reconnected because of this second near-death event in his life. There'd be no more slow southern drawl out of that boy's mouth.

With newfound speed, he explained, "We'd just missed the cabin cruiser thanks to Dave C.'s maneuver. About ten seconds later we hit the rock pile which tore the boat motor off Dave C.'s boat and sent us flying into the lake. We made it back to the rock pile, but Terry didn't show up until sunrise. Dave C. rescued him."

Turk piped in, "My ass hit the water at breakneck speed. Took all morning for it to drain."

Turk's mixed metaphor raised a few eyebrows. It sounded farfetched, but you could get water up your butt when you hit a lake surface hard. That happened to me once when I fell bottom first trying to waterski barefoot at high speed. Enema city.

I moved the conversation on, "What about Dave C.'s boat and motor?"

Turk answered, "Dave C. is a smart man. He had insurance on the boat. He'll have to pay for the salvage to get it off the lake, but he'll get enough insurance money to get another boat."

We of the tribe sipped our beers in unison, contemplating Dave C.'s business savvy. He impressed us yet again.

Dave C. was not at the get together that night. He was out walking the two-lane. He needed to be by himself to sort things out. It was one hell of an event, the crash and all. It really shook him. He was an amateur boxer for a while in his teens. He learned then what it meant to get pounded into the ground and recover. Sometimes it took baby steps for a comeback. But with his tenacity it wasn't long for those tiny steps to turn into the rapid dance of a boxer renewed. Tomorrow he would start recovery. Next week he would have a new boat.

Given all the excitement of the day, no one felt like making it an extended stay. With some wrap up conversation we called it a night, finished our beers, and headed to bed in various cabins, paired by love, or flying solo by fate. Interesting dreams would follow of launching bodies, draining Turks, fast-talking Scotts, and a floor of spent bottle caps that shouldn't have been there.

Chapter 20 - In the Dark

After the rescue recount, I headed back to my cabin to knock off for the night. The path I walked was lined with tall pine trees that shrouded the surroundings in darkness. A river of night stars flowed at the tree tops, mimicking the walking path's course.

I could see silhouettes of my fellow workers ahead. Their shapes were defined by faint light coming from the Lodge in the distance.

As I went along, I pondered my upcoming encounter with Wendy. We were to meet mid-morning tomorrow at the rope swing.

What would I talk about with her? Being outgoing didn't come naturally to me. I had a moment of qualm thinking my shyness might limit our conversation. Then I remembered something my dad Frank told me. He said, "With a new person, be interested, not interesting." Since I knew little about Wendy, being interested was the ticket. Words would come easy with that approach. The qualm subsided.

The starry clear sky above suggested that it would be a sunny morning. The outdoors would be good to share with Wendy. Confidence about our get together took flight.

My pondering had put me well behind my silhouetted friends. As I moseyed, I sensed someone on my left.

"Davie." It was Lisa. Because of the darkness, all I had to go on was her voice and a fragrance she wore. I knew the voice but not the fragrance.

She touched my left hand. "I'm scared of this path at night." She clasped a few of my fingers and held tight.

"Yah, it spooks me too. Let's chance it together."

Lisa smiled into the darkness. "I'd like that, thank you," she replied politely in her Boston accent.

We continued side-by-each at my lazy pace.

After a moment of quiet, she adjusted her hold, so our two hands were fully intertwined. Her hand was dry and cool. In some subtle way, her hand felt in charge of mine.

I was a bit speechless having this ex-girl of my dreams next to me. She walked close causing the back of my hand to nudge her hip with every step.

Lisa's hip movements brought Horhay and the boys to attention. Horhay and the boys were my penis and testicles. I named them that in Junior High just after I had the astounding experience of mastering their purpose. I think it was the day in Spanish I, when Senorita Anderson explained that "Horhay" was the phonetic pronunciation of "George." That night, the Senorita's figure, and her words of Horhay, became one with my unit, and the name stuck.

Since then, it never took much to get Horhay and the boys aroused – like repeatedly glancing off a girl's hip for example or eating cornflakes at breakfast.

Being preoccupied with Horhay, plus Lisa's fragrance and her physical closeness, made it difficult for me to tee up a coherent thought. I was hoping Lisa would fill the gap.

She provided the conversation rescue. "Quite an adventure the boys had. They were so lucky. I would have been so sad if anything had happened to them."

I came out of my hip coma to agree and threw in the fact that I had almost gone along.

She said, "That would have made me doubly sad, Davie. I think you are a special guy. Everyone likes you. Fred Laszlo even said you're the hardest worker in the place."

The praise from Fred Laszlo got my attention. "Where'd Fred say that?" I asked.

"He mentioned it to me after you'd finished bussing the dining room by yourself yesterday," Lisa replied.

"That's cool to hear," I said.

We'd come to the turn to her place.

"Well, it's true. You're a good guy, Davie. And thanks for not spreading the word about Maria and me. I know you saw us together."

"What are friends for?" I said.

"Exactly my friend," she said. "See you in the morning."

She gave my hand a squeeze and parted for her cabin door.

The space she no longer occupied next to me made a lonely void. I missed her immediately. Man, what a rollercoaster of emotions I rode with that girl from Boston.

"Good night, Lisa," I said as she turned to silhouette.

And to myself I thought, "Sleep tight, my friend who is a girl."

Chapter 21 - To Be

Romance was in the air.

The band began a slow dance, their first soft rock song of the night. Spotlights above the stage cast a hazy blue light over the band members and out onto the dance floor.

Terry put his hands around Wendy's waist. He smiled, thinking of their chance encounter at Madden's a few days ago, and their meeting that evening at Grand View.

In response to Terry's advance, Wendy put her arms tenderly around his shoulders. His athletic build was apparent. His muscles were hard, even at rest.

Wendy had a firm physique as well, but feminine in all regards. Regards that Terry found very appealing.

A few notes into the dance, she pressed her body into his and followed his lead. He moved one hand to the small of her back and swayed the two of them slowly.

The dance floor was crowded so they held together, not venturing beyond a few feet. They savored the intimacy of their limited space.

Terry looked deep into Wendy's eyes, and once again walked to the edge of the cliff. He felt ready to fall into thin air. Her newness was exciting. The urge to be wrapped in a prolonged embrace with her added a dimension of sensuality to their movement.

Wendy rested her head on Terry's shoulder. She held him closer. The heat was on. Terry closed his eyes and inhaled the scent of Wendy's hair.

"Terry. Wake up son."

Terry opened his eyes groggily. Wendy's caress evaporated. Instead, he was confronted with Dr. Spanker's paunchy face, the face of the Brainerd hospital doctor that had tended to him since the boat crash. Ah yes, the boat crash.

Terry took in his surroundings and found he was still horizontal in bed, versus dancing romantically upright with Wendy. Pain meds had kept his injuries in check, and they had apparently influenced his dreaming too in a most pleasant way. He longed to slip back into the dance, but Dr. Spanker kept on.

"So, Terry, tests show no internal damage from the crash. Your collarbone and ribs will heal up fine; however, it will take a few weeks," the doctor said. "Time for you to go home. You'll heal better there among your family."

Terry replied, "Well that would be my family at Grand View Lodge. I'm a summer worker there. My real family's in Mobile, Alabama."

"You must know the Laszlo family then. Good people. They'll take care of you," said Dr. Spanker as he finished up the paperwork on the clipboard tethered to the end of Terry's bed. "Call your folks from the phone there and let them know what's going on. Then you're free to go. The nurse will see that you get a ride back to Grand View."

That was good news. Terry was anxious to go. The overnight stay in the hospital was a boring affair. He wanted dearly to find Wendy and make their dance real.

"Sounds good. Thanks doc."

The doctor nodded with a smile and took his leave. Terry eyeballed the phone. Yesterday Fred Laszlo told the hospital admissions clerk that Grand View Lodge would cover the entire cost of Terry's hospital stay. Since money wasn't an issue, Terry thought, "Why bother the folks with my minor brush with death?" He skipped the call.

Terry got up and dressed on his own. He had trouble getting the sling onto his bad arm because his collarbone was still inflamed. But he worked through the pain and figured it out. He knew he had to do so on his own, so then was the time to start.

The nurse came in shortly after with a wheelchair. She had the remainder of Terry's pain medication in a pharmacy bag. With that he was good to go. He chose to walk on his own to the hospital lobby for the ride back to Grand View. It felt pretty good to be upright although he was feeling weak from inactivity.

The nurse had summoned Fred Laszlo. That meant a smooth Cadillac ride home. Fred showed up thirty minutes later and off they went. The Caddy launch was subdued. Fred knew to respect the hospital quiet zone and did so. When they hit the two-lane though, he put the pedal to the metal, like old times, and flew.

Terry enjoyed the freedom of the fast ride after being cooped up in the hospital. They took the curve around Hole-in-the-Day lake at seventy miles per hour. That speed put them at the Mobile boys' cabin in twenty minutes.

Seeing the cabin, Terry felt happy to be back. He said. "Thanks for all your help Fred. I really appreciate it."

Fred said, "No problem son. The Laszlo family sticks together eh?", implying Terry was a member. "Take the day off and get back in working order. Tomorrow too if you need it. Consider the days paid leave."

"Nice! Will do Fred. Thanks again."

Fred left Terry in a cloud of Caddy dust as he departed, and Terry turned toward the Mobile boys' front door.

It was still early morning and Terry had the whole day off ahead of him. Denny and Scott were at work, so he had the cabin to himself. As he entered, it looked perfect for the rest and relaxation Dr. Spanker had prescribed. Home sweet home at last.

Chapter 22 - Quiche

After my late-night walk with Liza, I had gone right to my cabin and directly to bed. I wanted dawn to arrive as soon as possible, so I could get on with seeing Wendy. I slept great until the Westclox alarm rang me to my feet. I showered myself awake, then dressed and went straight away to the staff dining hall for breakfast before the morning dishwashing shift.

Staff breakfast was always delicious, prepared right from the Lodge kitchen – usually a hot entrée choice like spinach quiche that morning along with other fare you prepared yourself. The Laszlo family knew that well-fed employees were happy ones.

I went for the quiche, peanut butter toast, cantaloupe slices, and OJ. I then parked myself next to Annie. She was a quiche fan too, I noted.

Annie smiled and said, "Hey Dave, you look happy this morning."

"Well, I have a potential date today with a real girl," I replied.

Annie's eyebrows arched up. "A real girl, eh?" she asked, emphasizing the word real.

"Yes, a real girl. I'm tired of imaginary ones."

"Well, I know girls around here that would qualify as real. Anyone I know?"

"She's a guest. Her name is Wendy. She sits with her family at table nine in the dining room."

"Oh, yes. She seems very nice. So does her family. How'd you meet her?"

"She was out front on the tree swing writing in her journal yesterday as I came by. We talked a bit before she left for the beach to meet her folks. We agreed to meet this morning, same place to talk again."

Annie's face went serious. "We aren't supposed to date guests, Dave. That could get you fired."

"I know. But where does a conversation with a guest fall within that rule? Grounds for dismissal?" I sounded like the lawyer Perry Mason on TV.

"Well I can see you've thought this through. Would what I say make a difference?" Annie's skepticism was lighthearted.

"I take your words very seriously, Annie. But the potential for true love rules. The conversation is on for just after my shift."

"OK sir. We'll see where fate takes you. Let Rob and me know when you get fired, so we can help you get a ride back to the Cities."

We both laughed at the possibility. The shared humor, with the undercurrent of risk, created a momentary bond that reflected in our smiles and eyes. Little dots in time such as that one were the molecules of our friendship.

With the start of our shifts approaching, I exclaimed, "Chow time," and polished off the rest of my food. Annie followed suite, and we left for our workstations, full of good food and thoughts to ponder during our waiting on the guests and washing of their dishes.

Chapter 23 - Fly By

Boredom set in shortly after Fred dropped Terry off. The cabin was just too quiet for Terry without his fellow Mobile boys there raising Cain. And he was wide awake. His hospital rest had seen to that. He felt he had the stamina for a walk. Seeing the grounds would do him some good.

He popped two pain pills just before exiting the cabin. As an afterthought, he popped a third one for fun. Being high would make for a nice day off. The breakfast shift was almost over, so he would likely run into his buddies. In the meantime, he'd walk down to the Lodge beach hut to catch up with Dave C. and Turk about the boat crash aftermath.

Terry cut by the tennis court which was empty. That was unusual for such a sunny windless morning. The court was silent without the pop, pause, pop of a tennis ball being volleyed back and forth.

The calmness of the court, combined with the pain pills kicking in, made the scene feel intensely peaceful. Ah yes, the pain pills. Terry suddenly felt quite right standing there.

Everything looked vivid, sharp in detail – the green surface of the court with its brilliant white boundary lines; the tall silver fencing reaching for the cloudless sky.

A second vivid thing caught his attention. He saw Wendy off in the distance on the rope swing in front of the Lodge. And I was approaching Wendy with a smile on my face that suggested our encounter was more than casual. We were about to trade greetings in a very natural, at-ease way, like we knew each other.

Terry chose to hang back for a bit to see what conversation ensued.

Wendy was as beautiful as he had dreamed early that morning. Fair skin. Long dark hair. A killer body that she thoughtfully dressed. She was the whole package when it came to attractive.

The talk between Wendy and me did not taper off. Terry began to get jealous.

"Wait a minute," he said to himself. "I met her first and we definitely connected. What's she doing with that kid Davie? Seriously? OK, time that an older more handsome man swept her off her feet. Me for example."

Terry's high reasoning overlaid his jealousy with self-confidence. He started on his way to make the sweep.

Chapter 24 - Meeting Two

In preparation to meet Wendy after my morning dishwashing shift, I had snuck into the Lodge Men's locker room to clean up. The locker room was off limits to Lodge staff, but it saved me a trip back to my cabin, so I took a chance to slip in and out. Plus, it offered fresh towels, manly soap, toothpaste, and toothbrushes. When done, I rolled out of the locker room unnoticed, looking good, and smelling of English Leather cologne.

Annie had given me the heads up earlier that Wendy was with her family for breakfast. With Wendy in the vicinity and me pulling off the locker room cleanup, the stars were in line for our rendezvous. I was riding high on adrenaline.

I went through the Lodge Great Room headed for the front door. As I exited the Lodge, Wendy was there on the rope swing waiting. I couldn't help smiling. I let the big wooden screen door slam and sauntered down the Lodge porch steps hoping to catch her eye. I did, and she returned my smile.

"Hello Dave," she said. "How are you this morning?"

"Very good Wendy, and you?"

"I'm fine too. I had a good breakfast with my mom and dad. They took off to golf at Madden's with their

Minnesota friends, so I'm on my own for the day. What are you doing today?" she asked.

This was getting good.

"Well, I'm free until four o'clock when the evening shift starts. Then I am back to washing the dinner dishes until eight or so. I consider it an honor to clean yours, by the way."

Wendy laughed. "And how do you recognize my particular plate?"

"Well, it's the cleanest one of the bunch."

We both laughed.

"Groovy Dave. My younger brother's a dishwasher too at the nursing home in town. He got time off his job and is along on our vacation too. We all love it here," she said.

"Where are you from?" I asked.

"We live in Minot, North Dakota. I'll be a senior in high school this fall. You?"

"I live two hours south of here, as the crow flies. In St. Anthony Village, a suburb in the Twin Cities of Minnesoota." I put a Swedish spin on it.

Wendy smiled at the accent. "The Twin Cities?"

"That would be Minneapolis and St. Paul. They began as settlements a few miles apart on the Mississippi when Minnesota was born in the 1800's. They grew together into one large urban area over the decades. They're still two distinct cities though. Minneapolis is Chicago-like. St. Paul is more small-town."

"You sound like a teacher. I'm impressed."

"That was part of a speech I did last year in English. I called it 'My Home Towns'. I live on the border of each. I can stand in both cities at once if I straddle Highcrest Road nearby my house."

"You're cool to know that," Wendy said. "This resort is the farthest I've been from my hometown. I need to see the Twin Cities. Find out what big city life is about."

"You'd like it. I can tell."

"Really? How can you tell?" Wendy smiled right at me. Both of us delving straight into our personal lives felt awesome.

I was about to answer when I noticed busboy Terry walking toward us. He had a sling around his neck that was supporting his left arm. Oddly, he walked straight through the flower bed on his way to us, tromping the plants down and seeming not to notice.

There was looseness in his look. Too early in the day to be stoned I thought, but with Terry you never knew. He liked getting high. The hospital stay was a probable contributor to his current state of mind.

"Terry, you're back," I said. "What's up? How are you doing?"

Geez, it was sure a surprise to see him.

Wendy turned the swing to see who had joined us. She was surprised too, beyond just seeing someone new for the first time. She looked as if she knew Terry.

Terry greeted us both with a nice smile, "Hi Wendy. Hi Davie."

Chapter 25 - The Duel

I didn't know what to say. Terry was back from the dead and judging from Wendy's reaction, she apparently knew him.

"Hi Terry," said Wendy with a puzzled look.

"You two know each other?" I asked.

"Yes," Terry said. "We met at Madden's in the Kon Tiki bar the other night. Not long after that, I was in the boat crash."

"Boat crash? What happened, Terry?" Wendy asked. She was sincerely concerned.

Terry proceeded to fill in the details of the crash, his injuries, the night floating in the darkness, the rescue, and the hospital stay. He left out the romantic dream dance with Wendy.

"My goodness, Terry," Wendy said. "That's an amazing story. You had a close call with the hereafter."

"Yeah," I said to myself. "And I bet I know what he's here after."

Terry topped me in looks and age. And he had the sympathy card going with his injuries. If Wendy and I were going to be, I would have to win her over in the wit and winning smile department. I felt I had a head start there. Plus, I had heard my remarkable blue eyes were hard to beat.

I had a few worthy characteristics in my interpersonal tool bag. So, "Onward ho!" to romancing Wendy.

But before I could even get started on the "onward" part of "ho", Denny pulled up in the Lodge circle driveway next to us. He was in his GTO with the convertible top down. The roofless car looked sleek with its highly polished black paint and skinny chrome strip running its length. His hair wasn't windblown, so he hadn't had the GTO up to speed yet.

Denny had to talk loudly over the idle of the powerful motor under the hood, "Terry, Fred Laszlo told the morning shift you were back. As soon as I got off, I hopped in my car to track you down. How are you doing, buddy?"

Terry shouted back, "Better by the minute."

Realizing he was disturbing the Lodge peace, Denny shut down the GTO power plant. That made talking much easier.

Terry continued, "Denny, this is Miss Wendy. We met at Madden's the other night."

"I remember seeing you Miss Wendy. But I didn't have a chance to say hello. Nice to see you again," said Denny. The Mobile boys politely put "Miss" on every girl's name as was the protocol down South.

"Nice to meet you Mr. Denny," Wendy replied in polite reciprocation.

Wendy said, "Dave and I were just about to take a walk. He was going to show me the grounds. Would you like to walk along?"

Wow, nice save Wendy. That made me happy.

Terry looked at me with a bit of a blank stare but recovered quickly. I could tell he was not happy about the situation.

Denny piped in, "I'm making a run to Bar Harbor, so no walk for me. Terry you should ride along and fill me in, if you'd like to, that is. Davie and Wendy, you can come too. It's a nice drive."

Bar Harbor meant "liquor run." I didn't think that was appropriate for our guest, so I took control saying, "Thanks Denny, but another time. After our walk we were thinking of taking a pedal boat out. We'll see the sights from there. Perfect day for it."

Realizing he had been aced out by me for Wendy's attention, Terry said flatly, "OK you two, have fun. Let's go, Denny."

Denny fired up the GTO as Terry got in. They rounded the circle in a reined-in roar and headed out. Hearing the rumble of the GTO fade away toward Bar Harbor was music to my ears.

Wendy turned toward me with a coy look and said, "Pedal boat, eh?"

I replied, "Yes, as we agreed before our visitors arrived, if you recall."

We shared glances, enjoying our moment of spontaneous conspiracy. It was exciting to be so in tune with each other right from the get-go.

Wendy got off the swing and put her hand in mine. "I am ready for that walk now, kind sir. And on the way you can tell me why you're called 'Davie' around here, Mr. Dave."

Chapter 26 - First Walk

The Lodge property was bisected in the east by the two-lane road that surrounded Gull Lake. On one side of the road were the Lodge grounds with the Lodge, tennis court, guest cabins, and lake facilities. On the other side was the sprawling Lodge golf course with its long fairways dotted with brown sand traps, and its eighteen putting greens with skinny white pins sporting red flags to identify golf ball destinations. The ubiquitous half-century-old white pines provided guests with cool shade and pine-scented air for all their summertime pursuits. The Lodge owners conceived this marvelous getaway destination decades ago, and nature filled in the blanks as each decade took its turn.

Wendy and I had plenty of territory to roam in any direction. We chose west and set out for the beach. The Lodge white pines were our chaperons. They felt the positive vibes we were emitting, and they swayed in approval. Pines are sensitive beings.

I told Wendy, "This coming school year, I'll also be a senior at my school, St. Anthony Village High. Home of the Huskies."

Wendy stopped dead in her tracks. "No way. My school is Home of the Huskies too!"

I chuckled. "Well we're the same age, appreciate good writing, and share the same school mascot. We've been living parallel lives."

"And now you and I have proven that parallel lives can intersect," she said brightly.

"So, our meeting bent the rules of geometry. I'll have to tell Mr. Pruist that when I get home. He was my geometry teacher in ninth grade. He'll get it. He's a true hippie. Very not square. He wears paisley ties and has hair down to his shoulders. He drives a Volkswagen van too with peace signs front and back."

Wendy smiled. "He sounds like my English teacher, Miss Plotnik. I can talk with her about anything. She always sees the possibilities, not the rules. She encouraged me to write."

We walked on. As we approached the Lodge beach hut, Gertie got up from her post on the corner and did her three-legged jaunt to meet us.

I did introductions. "Hello Miss Gertie. This is guest Wendy."

Wendy stuck out her hand, so Gertie could register her scent. I noticed Wendy's fingers were mindfully tucked in. She knew how to greet a strange dog and not get a finger nipped, not that Gertie would ever contemplate such a thing.

Gertie nuzzled Wendy's hand, and Wendy followed with a vigorous pet saying, "Hi Gertie. Very nice to meet you."

Gertie looked over at me and smiled approvingly. She said, "Wendy's a keeper, Davie."

I thought back, "Indeed, Gertie. Indeed." Gertie's judgment was right on as usual.

"Gertie is the Lodge dog," I explained. "She's the fastest dog around on three legs."

"How'd she lose her front one?" Wendy asked.

"Chasing a car on the two-lane out front. Her leg caught the rear tire of the car and had to be amputated. Very sad, but she made a great comeback," I replied. "She's still surprisingly fast."

"That's so cool. Hey, this is a nice spot. Let's sit for a minute. Take in the grand view."

Gertie and I shared a chuckle at Wendy's play on words. What a witty girl she was.

"OK with me," I said.

We were at a wooden blue bench, shaded by the Lodge beach hut awning. It was a double wide, perfect for the two of us to sit comfortably close. Wendy and I took roost on the bench's smooth blue paint as Gertie assumed alpha dog position on the turf in front of us. We three had a wide view of the beach. At its center was the dock that ran out to the Lodge ski boat, all sleek and angled forward ready for action. The swimming area was defined by a large semicircle of white and blue buoys. A sign just beyond the buoys warned "No Swimming | Water Ski Area." In the middle of the swim area, kids were climbing a tall water slide and careening down its curves to a screaming big splash finale.

Wendy nudged me, "Good job, Mr. Tour Guide. A view with a water show included. Nice planning."

I put my arm around her shoulder and replied, "And let's not forget the upcoming pedal boat excursion."

We sat for a while and talked about our lives. Since our states bordered each other, there wasn't much radically different in our lifestyles. We were raised by hard working parents – dads that worked long hours to keep roofs over our heads, and moms that specialized in midwestern comfort food of meat, potatoes, something green, and Jell-O. We had wardrobes determined by the same four seasons. I joked, "Yah sure, up here in da Nort dars nine months of winter and tree months of bad sleddin'." Gertie rolled her eyes, having heard that one from me more than once, but Wendy laughed. Besides our common lifestyles, she and I shared the same dry midwestern sense of humor.

The arm I placed on Wendy's shoulder had fallen dead asleep while we chatted. I did not want to move an inch from her body, so I toughed it out as best I could. As gangrene was about to set in, Wendy suggested we check out the pedal boats. Thank God. Hand saved. Off we went, leaving Gertie snoozing in the midday sun.

Chapter 27 - Pedal Boats

Turk was tending to the Lodge boat rental when Wendy and I entered. He looked up from his *Guns and Ammo* magazine and greeted us with, "Hello Davie. Hello Wendy."

Wendy looked flat out surprised. I am sure I did too. Leave it to Turk to create an immediate mystery. How could he know her?

Inquiring for us both, I asked, "Turk, how do you know Wendy?"

"Two of the Mobile boys were down here half hour ago in their hot rod GTO talking to Dave C. and said you had a new girlfriend named Wendy. That kind of news travels fast in our Mecca of decadence." With a wink in his eye, he added, "I assume this lovely lady goes by that name."

Wendy caught on and joined the game. "Yes, that would be me." She took over the small room with her cool poise. "Thank you for the compliment, Turk. But I must say that Dave and I have just met. Too soon to call me girlfriend."

Wendy seemed so mature in dealing with Turk. That was a bit intimidating. She was at his level or above, while I always felt like a kid around him. In watching their interactions, I realized it was time for me to focus on being older, time to rise to the occasion of Wendy. I laced on my boots of maturity. Standing tall, I looked Turk straight in the chin and said, "Turk, we're looking for a pedal boat. Any available?"

"Nope," he replied. "They're in use for the afternoon. That big family from Duluth has all three out. Their goal was out to the rockpile and back. Good luck with that." Turk shuddered at the thought of visiting the crash site again.

To the rockpile on a pedal boat was an all-day endeavor. The craft was an unwieldy affair that had a bench seat mounted high on a pair of pontoons, with two sets of pedals for propulsion. It was slow going and a bitch in the wind. It was better suited for a short jaunt out to deep water for a dip, and then back. Good luck to the Duluthians indeed.

Turk continued, "The Old Town is all we have left for a crew of two. Otherwise you're talking a fishing boat and motor and some cash. The water's calm. The Old Town will get you around fine if you don't mind paddling."

"The Old Town is the Lodge canoe," I explained. "Vintage 1940."

"That sounds like fun, Dave," said Wendy. "I've never been in a canoe before. Let's do it."

"OK, Turk. One Old Town to go please." I said.

Turk grinned and said, "OK Captain Johnson, have her back by sundown."

"Will do, Turk. And the canoe too," I replied. "Wendy, your yacht is waiting. Follow me please."

We turned and headed for our maiden voyage. Turk went back to his *Guns and Ammo*.

Chapter 28 - Old Town

Wendy and I got the Old Town down to the lake by each grabbing an end and carrying it across the sandy beach. It was light and easygoing. We kept our footgear on to keep the sunbaked sand from burning our soles. At water's edge I popped my tennis shoes off and threw them in the canoe. Wendy did likewise with her sandals. By chance, we were both in shorts and t-shirts, perfect for comfortable paddling.

We waded the canoe into shallow water to avoid bottoming out when we got in. The sandy lake bottom felt nice and cool between our toes.

"OK, Wendy," I said. "To start, you'll sit, and I will paddle you around, so you get to know the craft. It can be tippy until you get a feel for it. Put your life cushion against the rear seat thwart." I pointed aft to indicate where. "Then get in and sit on the bottom with the cushion as a backrest."

Wendy said, "OK, but I want to paddle you around too, once I see how it goes."

"Absolutely. That was my plan as well," I said. "Heck, I'm not doing all the work."

We shared a smile.

I stood in the water, holding the canoe gunnels in a cross-armed brace so Wendy had a stable platform to step into. She positioned her life cushion as I had advised, got in gracefully, and sat down on the canoe bottom facing me.

"Very comfortable, Captain Dave," Wendy remarked. She arched her back on the cushion and crossed her legs modestly, creating a visual double entendre that said get in the canoe now Dave.

And so I did, with Horhay at half mast.

As all systems were go for launch, on more than one front, Wendy looked puzzled. "Aren't we kind of in the wrong spots?" she asked. "Shouldn't we be sitting in opposite seats?"

Relieved her puzzlement was not boner related, I explained that when you paddled solo, you sat like I did, reversed on the forward seat. That put you more toward the center of canoe for better balance and control. And it kept the canoe level.

"Makes wonderful sense," Wendy remarked. "I'll remember that when I do the paddling for your sightseeing pleasure."

I winked in approval, grabbed my paddle's shaft, and took us out beyond the boat dock into open water. The Old Town glided us easily there.

Chapter 29 - Sea Ray

While Wendy and I were getting our Old Town canoe underway, Dave C. and Rob were across Gull lake at Madden's checking out a '65 Sea Ray speedboat that one of Madden's guest had for sale. Dave C. got wind of it from Deputy Sheriff Thomas when the Deputy interviewed him the day before about his Glastron crash. The Deputy knew about the Sea Ray from his son who fueled guest boats at Madden's marina.

The story was that it's owner Bill was heading home to Wisconsin in two days and wanted to trailer back a wad of cash instead of his old boat, so he could buy a bigger Sea Ray from his wife's cousin's neighbor in Eau Claire.

Dave C. hadn't anticipated getting a replacement for his Glastron so quickly, but the Sea Ray situation sounded too good to pass up. It was a reputable boat with an owner anxious to sell and time running out. He smelled a sweet deal wafting from the west.

Dave C. lined up a viewing with owner Bill for the next day, courtesy of the Deputy's pump jockey son. He had enough cash on hand with funds from his used boat motor business, and he could verify the new boat for soundness and speed by himself, but he needed someone to pull around the lake on skis to see how capable the boat was for water skiing. That morning he rounded up the best water skier in sight, Rob, and the two of them got to Madden's marina as scheduled, thanks to Alonzo who always left the keys to the Lodge beach buffet truck in the ignition.

At the dock, Dave C. sized up Bill and his Sea Ray. Things looked good. Bill had dollar signs in his eyes. He wanted the boat sold. The Sea Ray was a well-cared-for beauty, comparable to the old Glastron in power, but beyond it in looks and appointments. Dave C. knew on the spot that he was buying the boat, although his poker face said no such thing.

After brief introductions and some background information from Bill, Dave C. said, "Well, I'm interested, but I need to drive it to know. OK if Rob and I take it out and see what it can do?"

Bill's eyelids closed and opened with a faint cha-ching. He followed with, "No problem, boys. Try skiing if you like. The equipment's all onboard."

"That would be great Bill," Dave C. replied. "Rob, you up for skiing?"

"Absolutely. Let's proceed," Rob replied. Rob lived to ski. The lake had some chop, but it was even and would present no problem for Rob. He was ready for it.

They boarded the craft, verified the ski gear, then took their spots, with Dave C. driving and Rob riding shotgun. Bill stayed on the dock to let the boys determine things on their own. They looked trustworthy enough he thought, plus it might expedite the sale. He cast them off as Dave C. fired up the Sea Ray. Once past the marina, Dave C. opened the throttle. The boat responded immediately with its hundred horses. The bow rose up as the propeller bit water, then the craft planed out fast to top speed. Quiet power emanated from the Sea Ray's inboard engine compartment – a big improvement over the Glastron's deafening outboard, currently at rest on the sandy bottom of Gull Lake

Dave C. smiled at Rob. "Good ride," he yelled. Rob smiled back. It was indeed. They had lucked into a very good boat.

At the middle of the lake, Dave C. powered down the Sea Ray to prepare for waterskiing. Rob donned a ski vest and jumped in the lake. Dave C. tossed in the pretty good slalom ski they had found in the boat. Rob slipped it on and righted himself in the water. Dave C. went aft to throw him the ski rope. He twirled it over his head and let go. The handle hit near Rob, making it an easy grab. With boat, rope, ski, and Rob aligned, Dave C. hit it. The Sea Ray was up to the task. Its power popped Rob up and out of the water in just a few seconds.

"Yes...nothing better than raw uninterrupted power for a deep-water start," Rob thought, then cut hard left and escaped the boat's wake.

Chapter 30 - Waves

Wendy and I were chatting away as little waves lapped the sides of the Old Town. I had stopped paddling after fifteen minutes or so, putting us a few hundred yards offshore. A balmy southern breeze took over then, drifting us lazily along. We had the lake to ourselves for a private conversation, if we were so inclined.

Inclined was my plan. I joined Wendy on the bottom of the canoe, opposite her, by propping my life cushion against my seat thwart, sitting back against it, and dovetailing my feet with hers – not touching yet though, out of politeness. The canoe bottom felt cool and the gunnels provided comfortable armrests as we spoke.

We traded stories about our brothers and sisters. She had the younger brother who was along on the trip and an older sister that stayed home to work her summer job and take care of the family dog. I told her of my two younger brothers and two older sisters.

"So that makes us both middle children. We're the family peacemakers, as they say," said Wendy.

"I didn't know that," I replied.

"Yes, it's called birth order. First child – born leader. Middle child – peacemaker. Last child – risk taker. Those in between are a blend of traits on one side or the other," Wendy explained.

"How do you know so much?" I asked.

"I am very smart. And modest." Wendy laughed at herself. She touched one of my toes with hers. My heart beat a skip.

I joined her laughter. She was so appealing, I could've burst.

She continued, "The middle child can also be the 'lost child'. The one that gets no attention and becomes self-sufficient to survive. Ventures out on his or her own. Seeks it. Is that you Mr. Johnson?"

Come to think of it, that was close. I'd worked since I was thirteen to have my own money. I enjoyed being away from home more than being there. Past summers were spent on daily bike treks that took me miles away, getting back just in time for supper. I did love my family, but loved my growing independence too – with a passion.

"I'd say yes to being independent. And you Ms. ... hmm?" Holy dog, I realized I was in a canoe falling in love with a girl and didn't know her last name. That was a bit embarrassing.

Wendy laughed at my mental pause and filled in the blank. "Langer, Mr. Johnson"

"Ah, thank you Ms. Langer. And how did you know my last name?"

"If I recall correctly, Turk referred to you as 'Captain Johnson' back at the rental shack."

"Good ear. You make me smile, Ms., ahh...Langer was it?"

"Indeed, Captain."

We laughed at our wittiness. The waves lapped and laughed too, as waves do when wit takes the time to drift along properly. Too often wit goes by on breakneck speedboats too fast to be fathomed. Our wit was just the right speed, surrounding us with happy waves.

Unfortunately, our happy waves were about to change. Off to the west I noticed a speedboat towing a skier. The skier was cutting back and forth, leaving a wall of spray eight feet high on the outside of each turn. Boat and skier were heading at us, and I hoped to high heaven the driver was paying attention to where they were going.

Chapter 31 - Wetness

The speedboat veered away from our canoe at a close but relatively safe distance and headed north. I could see Dave C. at the wheel with Rob in hot pursuit on a ski behind. I had no clue how that could be, given Dave C. sunk his boat barely a day ago. What an odd coincidence.

Rob followed the arc made by the speedboat as it made its turn away from us. He was on the outside of the wake putting up a righteous wall of water. He straightened out thirty yards away and we traded surprised looks as he shot by. He smiled a crazy smile and gave Dave C. the hand signal to circle around again.

"Well I'll be. That was my friend Rob being pulled by Dave C., the guy Terry told you about this morning who was at the wheel of the boat crash. What they are doing out here right now is beyond me. And it appears they are circling back to say hello."

Rolling waves from their wake reached our canoe, rocking us gently side-to-side.

"Well, you guys are never short on dull moments it seems," Wendy replied. She looked uneasy.

I totally understood. The combination of Dave C. driving a fast boat and a crazed Rob requesting another loop meant one thing – a wall of water soon would be drenching us.

"OK," I confessed to Wendy, "this is not looking good. Rob loves to spray people when he's on a ski. We're sitting ducks now and we're going to get wet."

Wendy's eyes got big. "What if he crashes into us?"

"I doubt that. Rob's one of the best on a ski, and Dave C. will keep things under control."

Wendy sensed my confidence. She changed her expression to dubious, and with a half-cocked smile said, "Dave C. that crashed into the rockpile?"

That lightened the moment up. I half-cock smiled her back and said, "Well, this'll fill one of your journal pages for sure."

Our canoe settled back down but the waves around us did not return to happy. Crazed skiers always caused them angst. Rob was likely to send them to treatment.

We both looked west. Sure enough, pass two was in progress. Dave C. had circled a little closer than before and Rob was carving a curve in Gull lake that was sure to soak us.

As Rob passed by, we could see his tilted body squarely through the wall of water he was putting up. His shape took on fluid distortions as if we were viewing him through a pane of rippled old glass. The million beads of water that were in flight toward us held a marvelous rainbow of parsed sunlight. In my mind, this brief spectacular scene was worth the pending wetness. I hoped Wendy was feeling the same.

To our surprise, the anticipated rain of terror arrived instead as a gentle sprinkle. Rob had miscalculated his cut, putting us on the fringe of his intent. Rather than a torrent, tiny cool drops of comfort marked our bodies and canoe bottom with even distribution.

Thankfully, Dave C. and Rob did not attempt another hello. They roared out of sight as mysteriously as they had come.

Wendy and I relaxed back in our cushions. We looked at each other, touched toes, and laughed, savoring that rare sweet moment in life when adrenaline and relief commingle creating a lasting memory, a best time. We had unknowingly experienced our first such memory together.

We lingered for a while longer enjoying the return to calm, then Wendy said, "Captain Dave, take me back to port please. I desire dry clothes and Lodge food."

"As you wish, Ms. Langer," I replied and paddled us forthright to civilization's shore.

When we landed, I offered to put the Old Town and its gear away, so Wendy could be on her way to join her family for the night. She agreed but lingered for a moment. With hands clasped behind her back, she leaned toward me and asked, "Will I see you tomorrow at the swing?" I promised I'd be there with bells on. Maybe a whole bell choir.

Riding high on thoughts of tomorrow afternoon with Wendy, I got everything stowed vividly back in place, then went to my cabin to prepare for a vivid evening shift. That night the dirty dishes were the most vivid ever. Lisa too, flying in and out of the kitchen, was simply vivid. And my dreams later, oh my goodness, how vivid.

Chapter 32 - Thumbing It

The next morning arrived none too soon. The breakfast shift went by as usual, although I hardly remembered it because of my preoccupation with Wendy and what the afternoon might hold. I cleaned myself up again using the Men's Locker Room and left without a trace except for an ample scent of English Leather cologne trailing me.

Once out the Lodge front door, the wind immediately left my sails. Wendy was nowhere to be seen. I walked up to the rope swing. There was a piece of paper curled up and stuck through one of the rope loops. I pulled out the paper and unrolled it. Inside was a note –

Dear Dave,

I have to go with my parents today to Nisswa for lunch and souvenirs. I am really sorry that we can't see each other. I hope we can tomorrow. Let's try.

Wendy

Wendy had intelligent handwriting, neat as a pin. And she had drawn a little heart after her name. That touched my real heart. While I felt sad that Wendy was gone, I was happy that she wrote me to say so, and that she wanted to meet tomorrow.

I folded up Wendy's heart and put it in my wallet. I wondered, "Now what?"

Well...I could go to Nisswa myself for a chance encounter with Wendy. It was two miles away as the crow flies, and a little less than four miles as the cow walks. Flying was out since I couldn't fly. Walking would have to do. Quicker yet, I could hitchhike.

I headed to the two-lane next. Traffic looked light when I got there, so I had to decide between walking backward all the way to Nisswa with my thumb out or skipping the hitchhiking and walking forward there instead. I opted to thumb it for a while since there was no rush. After all, I did not want to interrupt Wendy's family outing too early. Plus, it felt good to be out strolling the open road away from the Lodge for a bit.

I proceeded with the hitchhiking. It wasn't five minutes before an old panel wagon truck pulled over. I ran up to it. I always ran to the ride when hitchhiking to not hold up the driver.

The passenger door handle was missing. The driver leaned across the bench seat and opened it from the inside for me. He was a guy about my age.

"Where you headed?" he asked.

"Going up to Nisswa," I said.

"I'm headed to Pequot Lakes, so that'll get you there. Hop in friend," he said.

I jumped into the cab, slammed the door, and settled into the seat amid a strong scent of marijuana smoke. Hmm...now this was going to be an interesting ride, I thought. I had yet to smoke pot. It was prevalent on college campuses and in hippy communities, but not in my neck of the woods. Pot was on Lodge property too, although under the radar. No one ever mentioned its use openly, but pot's distinctive aroma hung in the night air on occasion outside certain staff cabins.

"Hi, I'm Lucas. I live just the other way in a cabin on Gull. How about you?"

"I'm Dave. I work at Grand View. I'm from the Cities though. Go to school in St. Anthony Village."

"Cool," Lucas said as he got the truck rolling. "I'm from the Cities too, Robbinsdale. I live there when it's not summer. Hey, I've got half a joint left here. Mind if I smoke it? You're welcome to some too."

"Sure, smoke it. But not me, thanks." I had heard that pot could make you go crazy if it was laced with heroin. Lucas was acting normal, so the pot was likely just pot, but I didn't want to chance going psycho in front of Wendy's folks, just in case the heroin hadn't kicked in yet. So, I refrained.

Lucas lit up the joint and got the truck in third gear for highway speed. We had the green light at Schaefer's corner, so he double clutched down to second gear and rounded it smoothly. Then back up to third gear for points north.

The cab filled with pot smoke as Luca switched back and forth between working the joint and shifting the gears. He was skilled at both. Luckily so because he had to slow down unexpectedly to avoid a truck that was just barely off the road. The flatbed in back was full of metal scrap. Part of the load had shifted off and metal shards were strewn about on the shoulder. Also nearby was a dead deer we had to skirt, the result of it getting clobbered by the truck in a poorly-timed highway crossing attempt, or a well-timed deer suicide.

After we cleared the accident scene, Lucas took a final toke and stowed the roach in the ashtray. Now, I can't say for sure if I got stoned in the process, not knowing what stoned felt like, but man I wanted some French fries when we arrived at Nisswa shortly thereafter.

As I got out of his rig I said, "Thanks Lucas. Nice riding with you."

"You too, man. Take care." He gave me a smile and a wave and took off for Pequot Lakes.

Chapter 33 - Mug and Cone

Nisswa was the poster child of Minnesota tourist stops. Its main drag ran four blocks north and south and was appropriately named Main Street. The town businesses provided vacationers with authentic souvenirs imported from Japan, live bait and tackle, local specialty foods such as deep-fried green beans, and root beer floats in frosty mugs. Picture postcards bought at Totem Pole Gifts could be mailed directly from the post office at the north end of town.

Opposite the post office was the town dance hall. Friday and Saturday nights featured the house polka band and setups for adults that brought their own hard liquor. Wednesday nights had local rock bands from Brainerd for young adults. Soft drinks only though, no BYOB.

Lucas had dropped me at the south end of Main Street which was a short walk to the Mug and Cone root beer stand. It was a nice spot with a triangle of grass and a few picnic tables shaded by two big oaks. I decided to plant myself there until I had to head back to Grand View for the evening shift. I'd need an hour for the walk back which gave me half the afternoon for some food and people watching and maybe the encounter with Wendy.

I felt unusually ravenous, so I decided to splurge on a tall root beer and large fries. The lady at the root beer stand window gave me a smile as I walked up. Her name tag said Delphine, in loopy cursive writing. "Hello," said Delphine. "Are you ready to order?"

"Yes, I will have a tall root beer and a large order of fries. For here please."

"That'll be right up. Thirty-five cents please."

I dug into my jeans pocket, then handed Delphine exact change. I stood aside to wait for the food and glanced down Main Street. It was busy with midday foot traffic, but no sign of Wendy.

After a few minutes, I heard the cook in the back shout, "Order's up." Delphine organized a tray with a squeeze bottle of ketchup and napkins and slid the whole affair out the window at me.

The fries smelled great. I took the tray and said, "Thanks Delphine."

"Your welcome. Enjoy sonny," she said, then disappeared behind a screen that she slid across the order window to keep flies out. There weren't any flies in sight, but it was still a good precaution against that one lone bugger that lurks unseen, waiting to fly in and make a person who is normally profane adverse say, "Fuck, where's that fly swatter."

I set my tray on the picnic table that offered the best view of Main Street. The table put me in direct view of anyone approaching the Mug and Cone. Hopefully that would be Wendy sometime soon.

The root beer mug was heavily frosted, almost too cold to hold. And the fries were right out of the deep fat fryer, too hot to eat. The fries could be cooled with ketchup. However, I did not want to take the easy path. I wanted them hot and naked. I started the countdown to junk food ecstasy, that point where hot fries won't blister the roof of your mouth.

Point reached, I ate my first fry. It was a miracle of salty crispness. I followed it with a swig of cold root beer. All my taste buds had tiny concurrent orgasms. The rest was a blur. Head down, I ate, drank, ate, nonstop until the final fry. I swiped it over the wax paper basket liner and got the last of the ketchup for the perfect finish. I sat back fully satisfied thinking, "Now there's three dimes and a nickel well spent."

"Dave." I felt a touch on my shoulder.

It was Wendy. I was so absorbed with eating I hadn't noticed her approach. She materialized in one of those rare moments when you've set off for the unlikely and the unlikely does occur. I could've flipped.

"Well hello, Wendy."

"What are you doing here, Dave?"

"I hitchhiked here for a root beer and fries, and to find you."

"Find me so I could tell you that you have ketchup on your chin?"

"Yes. Do I?"

"Yes."

I wiped my chin with a Delphine napkin.

"Better?" I asked.

"Much," Wendy said.

"Well then, mission complete. Time to head back."

"What? Not so soon, please." Wendy sat down, pressed close, and clasped my hand.

Our impromptu play had no fourth wall. It was real, heartfelt. Written in the language of love.

"I saw you from down the street. So cool, you appearing from nowhere."

"I found your note. Thank you. It was great. I took a chance and came here. I hope you don't mind."

"Not at all. It was sweet of you to try. Would you mind meeting my family?"

"I'd like that. Let's go say hi."

I stowed my trash and put the tray back at the root beer stand window. Delphine gave me a knowing glance from the side window, as Wendy and I rounded the root beer stand corner. She knew by our clasped hands what was up. She saw it a hundred times every summer, lovers new to each other heading up Main Street anxious for their first kiss. "Good luck in love you two. I could sure use some myself," she said. "What, Delphine?" said the cook from the back. "Nothing Henry. Hey, you want to come over tonight?"

Chapter 34 - Family

Wendy and I found her mom and dad at Totem Pole Gifts perusing postcards in the wire frame postcard rack. Her dad was eyeballing a postcard with a fisherwoman on a dock exhibiting her pair of record size yabos and a large walleye pike too. Yellow letters spelled out, "What a Keeper. Summer 1970. Gull Lake Minnesota."

"Hi mom. Hi dad," Wendy said.

Her dad quickly filed the postcard back under Humorous, turned and smiled at his lovely daughter. Then he gave me the once-over and said, "Where've you been and who's this gentleman?"

"This is Dave, who gave me the canoe ride yesterday."

"Hello Mr. and Mrs. Langer," I said.

Wendy's mom said, "Oh how nice to meet you Dave. Please call me Linda and this is Gerry."

Gerry held out his hand and I did too. We shook hands firmly, amiably. Gerry and Linda probably had eighteen years on me, likely mid-thirties. I could see where Wendy got her beauty. Both her parents looked youthful. You could tell they enjoyed life.

"So, you know canoes, Dave. Thank you for teaching Wendy. She had quite a bit to say about how it's done."

I hoped she left out the part about crazy Rob cutting by on the slalom ski. It appeared so since they seemed at ease with me.

"We had a nice time, sir."

Wendy cut in. "Dad, can we give Dave a ride back to the Lodge? He's on foot and needs to be back by four for his evening shift."

"Sure," said Gerry. "I think we've seen enough of Nisswa. Round up your brother and let's hit the road."

We found Wendy's brother leaning on the magazine rack thumbing through the latest *Hot Rod* issue. The cover page had an image of a GTO that could've been the Mobile boys'. It was car of the day for those into laying rubber in third gear on the straight away.

Wendy did the introduction. "Dave this is my brother, Sam."

Sam looked like a cute hippy work in progress, kind of a walking oxymoron of clean-cut counterculture. His lean fifteen-year-old body sported borderline long hair, the somber face of Jim Morrison of the Doors staring from his black t-shirt, shaggy rag stock blue jean cutoffs, and sandals made from tire retreads.

"Hello Sam," I said. "Good to meet you."

Sam parked the GTO back in the rack. "Hey, nice to meet you too. You the canoe guy?"

I looked at Wendy. She winked back at me. "I guess so," I said. I was getting a lot of traction with the family from that outing.

"Cool, man. Wendy, I'm bored. When we gonna get out of here?"

"Now, Sam. We're giving Dave a ride back to Grand View."

We turned and exited Totem Pole Gifts with Sam in tow. Wendy's folks were on the street sitting in a next year model Buick Riviera. The Riv was a long graceful sled of a car with two doors, and from there a radical wedge back that tapered to a rounded point at the rear bumper, beautifully aerodynamic and hardly a family vehicle. I was impressed with Gerry's priorities in road travel. The man was show and go for sure.

"Pile in kids," said Gerry. Linda slid over next to him, so we could flip her seatback forward and perform the pile in. Wendy and I dawdled so Sam would get in first, ensuring we would be next to each other. We ended up in the back seat in the desired Sam, Wendy, Dave order. Interestingly Linda stayed put next to Gerry in the front seat, creating an odd family double date configuration, with hippy Sam as chaperon.

Wendy's physical closeness reeled in my head and that of Horhay's too.

Gerry got the Riv back on Highway 371 south and to Schaefer's corner in a respectable three minutes. The light was green at Schaefer's and he took the hard right fast, pushing Linda into him and me into Wendy. Inertia and centrifugal force and Wendy's hip flat against mine brought Horhay to attention. Judging from Gerry's speed, I had two minutes to get Horhay to stand down before we graced Grand View's front entrance, or I would be in the embarrassing position every male teenager dreads – boner in view. I forced thoughts of things completely not Wendy – boat motors, why airplanes stay aloft, my grandma – nothing worked. Horhay insisted on staying erect.

Chapter 35 - Leaving

Gerry brought the Riv to a stop at the Lodge. "Thank you Langers for getting me back here on time. I really appreciate the ride," I said. Horhay stood firm. Oh God.

"You're welcome Dave. It was good to meet you before we left for home tomorrow," said Gerry. "Hope you have a great rest of the summer. Grand View must be a fun place to work."

Home tomorrow? I felt like I'd been knocked over with a lead feather. I looked at Wendy. She nodded a sad yes. To be polite I stayed in Minnesota-nice mode, but underneath I was feeling sad from the surprise of Wendy's looming departure. I replied, "Yes, Grand View is really fun. Like getting to meet Wendy and you all has been great."

I had just a few minutes to get to work. Shoot. My time with Wendy was evaporating faster than steam from a pot of hot. Wendy said, "I'll walk back to the cabin from here, so I have a minute with Dave before he starts his shift."

"OK sweetie," said Linda. "Bye Dave. Nice meeting you. Wendy don't forget about supper this evening at the Lodge."

"I won't, Mom."

I pushed the seat back forward, leaned to the passenger door handle, and opened it. Horhay's enthusiasm had subsided with the news. I got out of the Riv followed by Wendy. Her family rolled away in the direction of their cabin.

"Well, Wendy, I'm sad you're leaving so soon," I said. "We were just getting to know each other. I wish we had more time." I made a bold revelation. "I really like you."

"I'm sad too, Dave," Wendy said. "I will never forget that canoe ride. Can I write to you?"

"Yes. Please," I said. "We could continue the story we've started."

"I think you are a poet underneath, Captain Dave," Wendy said. "I need more of your words. I have nothing to write your address down with."

"I'll get it to you tonight at dinner. Annie can bring it," I said. "I have to get going."

"OK go dishwasher man. I'll look for your address tonight."

I spun and got my feet moving to the kitchen. Wendy turned and headed toward her cabin. She whispered, "Bye my new love" as she disappeared. Her words reached me, too faint for my ears to hear. But my heart felt them loud and clear, and the pines smiled with the knowledge.

Chapter 36 - Last Supper

On the way to the kitchen, I sidetracked to the Lodge front desk to compose the note to Wendy. Fred Laszlo was staring out absently from behind the desk, his daydream framed by two ornately carved dark wooden desk posts that rose and joined above his head. Leaving his Neverland, he greeted me with a cordial, "Hey Davie, what's up?"

"Starting my shift," I said. "Gotta write a note before I do."

Fred sensed a mission in progress. He enjoyed participating in staff lives, what little he could, so he shoved a notepad and pen across the desktop to me. "There you go son but make it snappy. You're running late." Although entertained by what might be, he kept his tone businesslike to maintain the Lodge staff hierarchy.

"Will do, Fred"

The note paper had *Grand View Lodge* printed in clean letters at the top, bookended on each side with swaying pines. Perfect I thought, as a reminder to Wendy of this wonderful place.

I carefully printed my name, address, and phone number, followed by "Canoe voyages upon request. Call anytime." I stowed the note neatly in my wallet next to Wendy's from this morning.

"Thanks, Fred" I said. He released me with a grand wave, as if sending off a homing pigeon with a message that lives depended on. How right he was.

I could not cut through the dining room. That was guest only territory. So, I exited the Lodge lobby, taking a hard left toward the kitchen back entrance. As I rounded the next corner I saw the Langer Riviera approaching in the distance. The Riv was too far off to make anyone out, but it was a good sign that Wendy would be dining at table seven tonight as I started in on the evening dishes. Knowing the likelihood that my note would find her made my heart beat faster.

I punched in slightly late for my shift. As I passed the cook line, Amile the chef said a terse, "Hi, Davie," and went back to carving a big ass ham. He didn't seem to mind my lateness.

I kept my eyes open for Annie as I fired up the dishwashing machine. A few minutes passed, then Annie swung through the dining room doors with her first order.

I got her attention over the din of the kitchen with a loud, "Hey Annie."

She looked back as she hung her order ticket on the cook's wheel. "What's up Dave?"

"I have a mission for you."

Annie came over, eyebrows raised. She looked busy, so I got right to the point.

I produced the note. "Please give this to Wendy, at the Langer table."

"Your new love interest, eh? Why can't you do it yourself?"

The dishwashing machine dinged, telling me it was time for Pavlov's dog to unload hot sterile plates from the machine's mechanical bowels. I lifted the Dish Exit Door bar with one hand and gave Annie the folded note with the other. A cloud of Wizard of OZ steam escaped the door, adding dramatic effect to the moment.

"She's leaving first thing tomorrow. I may not see her," I said. "Can you get it to her and say it's from me?"

"OK, Dave. But I hope Fred Laszlo is out of sight. You know the rule about fraternizing with the guests."

Ah, the "F" word again. Geez. "He's at the lobby front desk right now so you're in the clear. I'll owe you if you pull it off."

She nodded and left for her assignment.

I returned to my work, slipping my fingers automatically between four hot dinner plates, hoisting them up with one hand for stacking. The chrome wire rack that ran the length of the wall to my left would be their refuge until breakfast. They landed safely there.

Annie returned shortly with her second order ticket in hand. It was for the Langer meal. Along with it she carried a folded piece of paper. With a sweep of Swedish efficiency, she hung the ticket on the cook's wheel, slipped me the paper saying, "True love reigns," then danced back through the dining room doors for her next order, all in a blink.

I could hardly wait to read what Wendy had written. But I had to pocket the note. Between the Mobile boys' table clearing and Alonzo's pot and pan runs, I had a mountain of dishwashing piling up. I stowed the note in my tee shirt pocket, next to my heart for safekeeping.

The next two hours would fly by. Friday nights always did. We were extra busy, as most guest families made sure to have their last Lodge supper before leaving the next day, except for those lucky to be staying for another week.

They had the luxury to eat or not, knowing their time wasn't up yet.

Halfway through the dinner rush, my nemesis Terry popped his head through the bussing window. He was feeling no pain from round three of pain meds for the day and had convinced Fred Laszlo that he could do some light bussing. He startled me with, "Hey Davie, I asked Wendy out tonight as I filled the family's water glasses. She's all for it. Her dad said I could take the Riv, too."

Reflex kicked in and I shot a line of rinse spray at his face. He ducked back quickly, avoiding a soaking. On the off chance he'd reappear in the window with another taunt, I fired a second line of spray. My guess was right. He looked in again just as the spray arrived, nailing him square in the face.

Sometimes it is not a good idea to spray your nemesis in the face.

Terry had just topped off a pitcher of ice water before our exchange, making him armed (well...one-armed) and dangerous. He came flying through the dining room doors bent on revenge and launched the ice water at me. It floated in a dreamy arc of liquid and cubes until it took purchase on my chest with a big splash, drenching me cold.

Amile the chef caught the whole event from behind the cook line. He slammed down the pot he had in hand and approached us with rage spewing from his face. A calamity like this on his watch was unheard of. He stopped himself just short of ringing Terry's neck and yelled, "What the devil is going on here?"

Terry stood his ground. "This moron dishwasher just sprayed me in the face with rinse water."

Amile gave me a fuming look. I kept quiet. I'd found that stoicism during chaos is a powerful defense. Let your opponents babble on emotionally until they run out of babble, then finesse a peaceful outcome with some cool choice words.

I didn't need to speak. Amile chose to defuse the situation with, "OK you two. Back to work. I'll deal with both of you later."

We caught Amile's drift – no more argument. Terry and I looked smugly at each other before retreating to our stations to carry on as if nothing had happened. The guests hadn't seen or heard the fuss, so Amile's move was to keep all quiet. Anyone in the kitchen that saw the to-do caught Amile's drift too. They carried on as normal, but their pained glances at the two of us said we were screwed.

The evening dinner shift ended with no further turmoil. Terry joined me in the kitchen afterward for our reckoning with Amile. I stuck out my hand, saying, "Sorry Terry." We shook hands. Terry said, "Well, it was nice working with you, Davie." Our eyes met and conveyed the same thought – "What a couple of fuck ups." We laughed a good one at that.

Amile was nowhere in the immediate vicinity, which was puzzling. But he was a high-functioning alcoholic, so perhaps vodka had taken him out for a spin. After the ten-minutes-you-wait rule had passed, we high fived it and vamoosed. Discipline was going to catch up with us, but why ruin the rest of the night waiting? Besides, I had an important note to read.

I got outside and sat down on the kitchen loading dock with my legs hanging over its edge. The dumpster next to the dock smelled of rotting food. The night was mosquito heaven – cool and dark. Smell and mosquitoes be damned, I was going to read Wendy's note right then and there.

I took the note out from my tee shirt pocket and unfolded it under the circle of light that lit the dock. I was presented with indecipherable run-on blue ink. Terry's ice water had melted Wendy's gentle words into nothing.

"Holy dog," I said to the mosquitoes.

I could sort of make out two words: "goat noose." The rest resembled an accidental Wendy Langer watercolor.

Goat noose. Not much to go on.

Chapter 37 - The Kiss

OK it was time for some deductive reasoning. Wendy wanted to see me before she left. The note was her means to tell me when and where. "Goat noose" did not look like the when. Therefore, the words must have spelled out the where. The location had to be on Lodge grounds, if she was to see me before she left. First word, four letters. Goat. Boat. Ding. Second word, five letters. Noose. House. Ding-ding. I would find Wendy at a boat house.

Aha, *the Lodge boat shed!*

Now sounded as good a time as any to find out. I pushed off from the loading dock headed for the Lodge beach. The mosquitoes stayed put in midair. They preferred a stationary blood source, not one running away at top speed.

I slowed to a casual walk to catch my breath as the boat shed came into view. Clearing the boat shed corner, I found Wendy sitting on the overturned Old Town canoe. White shorts and tube top accentuated her figure in the twilight. I ached to hold her.

Our eyes met. There was no need for words. She stood. We embraced. We kissed.

It was a long kiss. A destination and a journey. One of those moments in love that defines loneliness to follow. How white defines black.

As we kissed, I made memory of the soft lace of perfume on the curve of Wendy's neck. She smelled clean, like Dove soap sprinkled with light cinnamon, floral and spice notes in sensuous accord.

We knew our time was short. We put everything we had into that kiss. It registered like a Sonny Liston punch in the kiss of all time.

We came up for air. Sweat cooled us naturally as the lake breeze found our bodies exposed.

What stopped us from getting totally naked was youth not knowing how to venture there.

"I have to go now, Dave."

Six words.

"I know."

Two words.

Then no words. The little time left was spent pressed together, memorizing secret places.

At last, out of time, we walked silently back to her cabin. Hands clasped. Again, no words. Touch spoke instead. We let our heated attraction for each other ride quietly on soft rails to the end.

Wendy and I kissed a final time at her doorstep, as prolonged as possible. Her dad's cough from inside the cabin ended things. We stared into each other's eyes and smiled, then let go. She promised to write as I turned to go. I started down the night lit path and heard the cabin screen door close delicately, and we were no more.

Chapter 38 – Gone

Gone is a painful word. Wendy was gone the next morning. We had parted the night before after our romantic interlude and her dad's cough. She and her family left at the crack of dawn, bound for home on the two lane that lead northwest to Minot North Dakota. Wendy was physically gone, but she was not gone from my heart. It ached when my brain said she was gone.

The dishes that morning were sympathetic. Sensing my heartache, they tried to come out of the dishwashing machine not so blasted hot. But they still stung my fingers. I appreciated their attempt.

Amile sensed my despair too. Looking through the cook line heat lamps he said, "Hey, Davie, you OK over there?"

I was glad for no mention of me spraying Terry in the face during our last encounter.

"Yah, Amile. Someone I just got to know had to head home today, so I'm bummed out."

"Ah, I get that. The good ones. They come and they go too fast in this resort life."

My shift was close to over. Seeing I was ahead on dishes and pots and pans, Amile said, "Go hit the road. Hitch to Nisswa or something. Have some of Delphine's fries. That'll make you feel better."

I smiled thinking of Amile maybe knowing Delphine firsthand. Small world, these north woods. I wrapped up the last load of dishes, and said, "Thanks Amile. I'm off like a prom dress. See you tonight." As I headed out the kitchen back door, he gave me a waved with his spatula and thought to himself, "First love of the summer. Always a heartbreaker."

The kitchen parking lot was hot as blazes for midmorning. I stripped down to my tee shirt. My jeans pocket held three quarters. I figured a trip for fries and root beer was within budget, so I pointed my aching heart toward Nisswa and prepared my thumb for the hitchhike.

The road to Nisswa was a barren expanse when I got there. From a stubby tree across the way, two big black crows were cackling to high heaven. I stood and listened for a few minutes. They were debating about how far it was to Brainerd, as the crow flies. The debate became heated. It was obvious each thought the other was way off. Finally, one gestured south and they took off to find out.

Peace restored, I surveyed my prospects for a ride. None were in sight. All roads in North America led to the very spot I occupied. Apparently at that moment everyone on the move was destined for spots other than mine.

The road's faded yellow line disappeared into a heat mirage about a quarter mile off in the direction I needed to go. As I looked, a gray ghost emerged from the mirage's watery sheet. The apparition was doing well over the speed limit, as apparitions like to do. Seventy maybe. It approached and rapidly took a familiar form – that of Lucas's old panel wagon with him behind the wheel.

Lucas flew by in a blur. I must have caught his eye because he hit the brakes and circled back. He overshot my position by ten feet with the brakes complaining of metal on metal.

I caught up to the open passenger window and heard him say, "Hey, St. Anthony."

"Hey, Robbinsdale," I replied.

"Dave, right? Where you headed?"

"Nisswa." I gripped the edge of the door window and looked in. The cab was worn thin with age but was neat as a pin. "What are you up to Lucas?"

"I was headed to Nisswa," he said with a shit eating grin on his face.

"Yah? Well you were going the wrong way man."

Lucas chuckled. "Yah? Well I'm pointed the right direction now, Want I ride? I have a full tank of gas and a whole fuckin' day to kill.

I gave him an "OK." He leaned over, opened the handleless door from the inside, and I hopped in.

Chapter 39 – Not Gone

Lucas got the panel wagon back up to seventy. We made the light at Schaefer's corner in no time and headed north on highway 371, bound for Nisswa. Looking from the cab back into the truck's interior, I spotted a crashed motorcycle roped to the floor.

"What's the story on the bike?" I asked.

"It is a '52 Vincent. For parts. I have a matching one back at the cabin that I am restoring." Lucas gave me a sideways glance to see if I was impressed. I was. It was a British bike, rare for these parts.

"Back-assward Brits. Shifter on the right. Brake on the left. Opposite from an American or Jap bike. Takes some getting used to. Scary if you get'em mixed up," he said.

I could picture it. You could get thrown into traffic pretty easily by hitting the wrong pedal and jolting the bike.

"Yah," he said, "but a few minutes on the bike and it comes back to you. Like riding a bike."

"Yah, like riding a bike," I said.

"Yah, like riding a bike," Lucas replied.

With that dead horse nicely beaten I took a gander back out my window. Ron and Mary's Car Repair and Oldé Café was passing by on the frontage road to the east. The building was a dilapidated white cinder block structure apparently designed in Depression times by an unemployed shoebox maker.

The repair garage and food café were kept apart in the front of the building by a wooden entrance door that had seen too many winter blizzards. Curls of green paint clung to its surface in survival-of-the-fittest randomness. Through the café picture window you could make out two booths and a six-stool lunch counter with some people milling about inside. Two orphan gas pumps graced the drive. A sign hung above them with big letters spelling "EAT GET GAS" to lure travelers off the highway.

As we got even with the garage door, it was open with a car inside on the hoist. I recognized the pointed rear window of the Langer's Riviera facing out. The Riv sat suspended in midair with a back wheel off.

"Holy dog," I said. "Hold it, Lucas. Stop."

"What's up man?" Lucas started deceleration.

"A girl I know is back there at Ron and Mary's place. I need to see her for a minute."

"Girl, eh? Nice. OK buddy. Will do."

Without pavement ahead to double back on, Lucas simply cranked the steering wheel hard right. That took us directly into the fuckerbrush of a shallow ditch that separated us from the frontage road. We exited the ditch, rattled but unscathed, and proceeded on to the garage. As we parked in the garage lot, Wendy's dad Gerry stood staring at two of the Riv's wheels that leaned against the cinderblock garage wall. Mechanic Ron stood by in greasy coveralls, delivering what looked like bad news.

"Replaced?" we heard Gerry say as we walked up.

"Yup," Ron said. "Holes too jagged. Tires wouldn't hold a patch past Pequot. I'll have to run down to Brainerd to get new ones. Warehouse has'em in stock. Eighty-five dollars total."

Gerry raised an eyebrow. "Wow. That's steep. Why so much?"

"The Riv has them new radial tires on it. Pricey. I could put on 4 ply's instead but you'd need four tires. Can't mix radials and 4 ply's. Cost ya the same either way."

Gerry kept his cool. He knew Ron had him over the stranded-tourist barrel. No point in dickering. "OK, do the radials."

"OK. I gotta job to wrap up in front of this. Adding in the trip to Brainerd for you, yours'll be done tomorrow noon."

"Tomorrow?" Gerry's cool receded a bit. "What'll my family and I do 'til then?"

"You can have the garage loaner. That'll get you to a motel for the night and back." Ron pointed to a rust-bucket Rambler sitting in a personal history of oil leaks.

Gerry caught Lucas and me looking on. "Dave. Hi guy. What are you doing here?"

"I saw your Riv in the shop. Lucas here was giving me a ride to Nisswa, so we pulled over. Everyone OK?"

"We're OK. About a mile back on 371 we blew both passenger-side tires. Wendy had spotted a deer and fawn. I pulled over on the shoulder to see'em better. Hit metal shrapnel from God knows where, and 'BOOM', the tires went flat immediately. Crawled the Riviera here and waited for Ron to open up. Looks like we're stuck here 'til tomorrow."

"Oh man, what a bummer," I said. Secretly though, my heart was tap dancing a Sammy Davis Jr. joy number at the chance to see Wendy again.

Lucas caught the drift of the situation and jumped in to help. "Hey Ron."

"Hey Lucas. How's the Triumph running?"

"Good. It's a Vincent though. Just scored some parts it can use." Lucas and Ron knew each other. They traveled the same motorhead circles in the area. Lucas continued, "Hey man, I can make the Brainerd run for you if that'd help. Be back here in an hour or so."

"Well that'd get the job done by supper."

Gerry piped in, "OK by me." He looked at Lucas. "I'd make it worth your while. How's ten dollars sound for your trouble?"

Lucas smiled. He could use the bread. "It's a deal man."

At that point, I caught Wendy watching me through the café window. I got a questioning look when our eyes met, then a big smile. I gave her a wave. She waved for me to come inside. Enticement flew a true arrow. I couldn't wait to get there.

Before long, the opportunity rose to head for the café. The men were talking details of the Brainerd run and didn't need me. I turned and made tracks for the flakey green entrance door. Delicious aroma of Olde burgers and fried onions seeped through cracks around the door's edge. Mary had a mess of half pounders sizzling on the grill for the Langer's lunch. I pushed the door open and entered. A brass bell on curled spring clanged, causing Linda and Sam to look my way. Wendy already had her sights on me.

"DAVE!" they all exclaimed.

"LANGERS!" I happily replied.

Chapter 40 – Lunch Too

I tried to look collected as I strode across the café's black-and-white checkerboard floor to their booth, but I was hopping excited to be in the same room again with Wendy. She was wearing a cotton dress dotted with tiny roses that called out her form in pointillistic fashion. I had to pull my eyes off her body to carry on the conversation.

Wendy said, "Dave, what are you doing here?" She was sitting next to Sam, with Linda on the opposite side.

Before I could reply, Linda said, "Sit down Dave, here next to me." She shifted over, then patted the vinyl space she had made.

I slid into the booth as kindly directed. I looked into the magnificent blue eyes across from me. Wendy's. She looked straight back into mine. Our souls floated together briefly, comingled. We kissed again in our imaginations. Got physical again. Good thing her mom wasn't a mind reader.

But Linda did not need to read our minds. She read the pause, our gaze, and knew what we were feeling. Moms know. She broke our spell with, "Yes, what are you doing here?"

I snapped to. "Well, I was headed to Nisswa with my buddy Lucas for a root beer and saw your car on Ron's hoist. You dad told me about the tires blowing."

Wendy said, "I feel bad. It was kind of my fault. I saw two deer. Dad pulled over so we could see them up close and the next thing we knew both tires on one side went flat. It was frightening."

"Man," I said. "What a bummer. But not your fault. The sharp metal on the road was to blame. Hey there goes Lucas." I pointed out the window. "He's going to Brainerd for your new tires. Sounds like you'll be back on the road late afternoon." The panel wagon farted blue smoke between second and third gears as it hit cruising speed. Lucas disappeared south down 371.

"Who had the California burger?" Mary stood by with four orders of burgers and fries lining her forearms. She was only four foot eight, so the burgers didn't have far to travel to reach the table.

"Dave," Linda said, "you can have the California. Gerry can reorder when he gets back in. We all get the rest of the cheeseburgers, thank you."

"Thanks Linda. I'm starving," I said.

"You're most welcome, Dave."

Wendy touched my foot with her toe. She gave me a surreptitious wink. I touched her foot back. Preoccupied with foot play, I don't remember eating the California burger, but it was gone in two minutes flat and my stomach was full. Hours since breakfast, everyone else devoured theirs too.

Gerry came marching into the café next. "Well, we have some time to kill. Car won't be ready for five or six hours."

Hearing that, Mary piped in, "You should take the loaner up to Pequot. Bean Hole Days is going on."

"What in the world is Bean Hole Days?" Linda asked.

"Two giant iron kettles named Thor and Big Bertha get filled with beans and buried in the ground on a bed of coals to bake overnight. They'll be opened up this afternoon. You go get some of them beans. Worth the trip. Turtle races and a camel ride today too. The whole shootin' match."

"Wow," said Linda. "Beans from a hole in the ground." She chuckled. "What are we waiting for? Let's go."

Sam's face replied with a half-enthused teenage expression. But his posture said he was in for it.

Wendy said, "That sounds fun. Can Dave come with? If you want to Dave."

"Sure," I said.

Well, Gerry thought, the Pequot event would definitely fill the gap left in the day from the tire fiasco. "OK," he said. "Let's pile into the loaner and go. Mary, what do we owe you for lunch?"

Mary grabbed the loaner keys from a hook under the cash register counter and tossed them to Gerry. "We'll settle up on the bill later. Have a good time family."

Chapter 41 – Pequot

Ron and Mary's loaner proved to be a great runner despite its rust bucket appearance. The Rambler's mechanical innards purred along with ease thanks to Ron's salvage skills and his attention to detail. We made it comfortably to Pequot in a half hour.

The town was named Pequot Lakes, but all the locals referred to it as "Pequot" to keep life simpler. Its three-block business district lead to the Bean Hole Days event at the town's American Legion park.

The only place to park was a half mile out on the highway, so Gerry pulled over and we hiked the rest of the way on foot. The split rail fence that surrounded the park was adorned with all colors of crepe streamers, making a festive ring around the hundreds of baked bean seekers. The renowned Chmielewski polka band umpa-umpa'ed from the bandshell. A real live camel plodded a tight camel ride circuit with its riders perched precariously high, swaying to the Chmielewski beat.

Wendy and I trailed her family as we went along. Thinking how nice it would be to hold her hand, I reached mine out a bit in search of hers. She caught my motion and joined hers with mine, then tugged me slightly off course from the family's path. "Mom, Dad," Wendy said, "we'll see you later. Dave and I are going for a walk around town."

"OK kids," Linda said. "Be back for beans before we have to leave so your tummy's full for the road."

"OK, Mom," Wendy said. "See you then."

Wendy and I slowed to a stop and turned around. We started back the way we came but found it awkward to walk two abreast against those heading to the event. The town's elementary school, not too far away, looked like a quiet destination so we got off the beaten path and headed toward it.

"Can you believe this? That we got to see each other again?" said Wendy, her eyes bright.

"So wild. Like unbelievable," I said, "I have some details about how it happened."

Wendy's eyebrows arched up. "Really. How?"

"Yesterday, Lucas and I saw an accident on the spot where your tires blew. A trucker had hit a deer and some of the scrap metal he was carrying fell on the shoulder right there. He didn't get it all picked up I bet. That's what did your tires in."

"Really? Wow!"

"Yup. Funny thing. If that trucker had missed the deer, you'd be almost home by now instead of here with me."

"I'm glad we're here for sure. Too bad about the deer though," Wendy said sincerely.

"Yah, deer get hit on that stretch all the time. Sad."

We meandered across the school's baseball outfield, holding hands as our talk continued. The smell of fresh cut grass registered the moment in our minds.

As we entered the infield, I ran the bases. Wendy stood by smiling, then tagged me out at third with a hug and a raucous "You're OUUUWT!" Sweat trickled from our pores as we clung to each other in the midday sun. We started to overheat.

"Hey," I said, "let's cool off somewhere."

Wendy nodded. "OK by me."

The ballpark dugouts held the only shade around, so we headed to the nearest one. Sunk halfway into the ground, it was a bit musty. Cobwebs hung here and there. We didn't care. The space was all our own, comfortable from the earth's coolness. We sat back on the dugout bench with our bodies close.

"Wendy," I said, "your family is so together. I bet you always have good times."

"We do mostly. But it is hard to be in the perfect family. My mom and dad always look perfect. They expect that from me and Sam. I can't breathe sometimes with all their rules. And I hear them fight at night about money, but they always seem to have enough for the new best thing. Sometimes I just want to run away."

"Really? That's a bummer. What do you do when that happens?"

"I get out because I sing in a rock band."

"Rock band. That sounds really cool."

"It's an all-girl band – the 'Jets.' I'm lead singer. We practice a lot in my friend Jenni's garage. We played our first gig in the Minot VFW talent show last May. Got pretty good applause which was exciting. We want to do more."

"Groovy. What songs do you know?"

"Two by the Rolling Stones, and one by The Doors, so far."

"Cool. I would really like to hear you."

"Well hitchhike to Minot, Dave. Let me know when you hit the edge of town and we'll make it happen"

I loved to hear her say my name.

"Ha! I just might."

Wendy's openness about her life spoke trust. I decided to open up to her. Take a chance about something serious along the same lines.

"My family looks good like yours, from the outside looking in. But my mom drinks and that's hard. She gets really mean and says mean things to me. Next day, all is normal. I never know what to expect after school. I never bring friends home. My dad just lets it go. I hole up in my room or wander around Apache Plaza until she's sleeping it off. She is so nice otherwise. It is crazy."

"Oh Dave, I'm sorry," Wendy said.

"You're the first person I ever told that to," I said.

That was true, and man it felt good to say it to someone who could relate. Get it out there. What the fuck. I found the weight of that miserable secret leaving my shoulders. For the first time in my life, I felt the sweetness of its release. I felt clarity. Renewal.

I squeezed Wendy's hand. She kissed me and I kissed back with cause. Our dugout was an oasis from the hard boundaries of right and wrong imposed by a confusing world. Our temporary freedom fostered a most lovely spontaneity, a place for us to share our passions without reservation. We took unencumbered advantage of each other. Rounded the bases. Found home. Sent innocence on its way.

Afterward, we rested in each other's arms and shared confidences until the shadows on the dugout wall told us we had to go.

Wendy and I made it back to her family in time for the last portions of Bean Hole Day beans. Linda filled us in on their afternoon, part of which included the polka-step camel rides. As we finished the last of our quite delicious beans, Wendy and I told her family of our conversation in the coolness of the earth sheltered dugout and how it led to our exquisite love making. Time had come to go. With full stomachs and our minds ruminating on stories just told, we hiked back to the rusty Ramble and piled in for points south.

I should confess, Wendy and I really didn't mention the exquisite love making part in words. A long-held glance between us did the talking.

We rolled into Ron and Mary's just as Ron tightened up the last lug nut on the new rubber. Job done on time as promised, Ron and Gerry settled the bill and shook hands.

All that was left was for us to say our goodbyes and part ways. I felt like walking back to Grand View. I was beyond late for my shift, so another hour wouldn't matter. I wanted time to contemplate what I would do next in case my job wasn't waiting for me when I returned to the Grand View kitchen. I had no good excuse for my tardiness, although in my mind I had the best of excuses. But that was for me to know. If I lost my job, maybe I would go live in Minot for the summer and be close to Wendy.

Gerry kicked off the departure with, "Let's get going kids. We have a five-hour drive to get home and it's been a long day. Dave, we'll get you back to Grand View."

"Thanks Gerry, but I'm walking back. No rush and it's a nice time of day for a walk."

Wendy came up to me, looked into my eyes, and said, "See you soon I hope." We hugged for the last time and I whispered, "OK, Wendy."

"OK, Dave," Wendy whispered back.

I wished them all a good trip as Wendy and I slowly separated. We exchanged goodbyes, then I turned and headed for Grand View on foot. I forced myself forward and got on my way.

I heard the Langers chatter as they boarded the Riv, the last of which included a faint "Bye Dave", followed by doors closing and Gerry's lead foot acceleration fading to the north. I took a look back and saw Wendy doing the same out the Riv's rear window. We shared a final wave, then became two dots of gone.

Chapter 42 - October

"Jesus, Mary, and Joseph," I said.

It had been a rainy night. I was standing under a dripping wet Pontiac, holding a wrench overhead that was one turn away from releasing a stream of hot black oil into the drain pan near my ear. Amid that, the gas station driveway bell went ding-pause-ding, twice, telling me I had to ratchet the oil plug back in and put on a rain slicker to gas up a customer's car. I was manning the night shift alone at Bob Springer's Union 76 gas station back in St. Anthony Village.

Cold rain pelted the slicker as I got to the gas pump island. The island was only a two-pump affair with one pump for Regular and the other for Ethyl. Besides selling gas, Springer's had two car hoists for oil changes and car repairs. Those were the money makers for owner Bob. People came in for gas, and his head mechanic Stosh sweet talked them onto the hoists for new shocks and tires.

Under the fluorescent lights that lit the drive was my mom Dorothy sitting in the family Oldsmobile. She peered out at me through swipes of the wiper blades. Light from the Union 76 sign above reflected in watery orange and blue rivulets down the car's hood. What an odd place and time for her to show up. There was a gas station closer to home with cheaper gas, plus it was after seven PM. All the stores in the Village were closed. Why she was out in this weather was a mystery to me.

Dorothy cranked down the window. "Hi Dave. Fill'er up please." She looked happy to see me. Sober too.

"Yes ma'am," I said with a smile. "What brings you here on this bad night, Mom?"

"A mail run." She sounded pretty US Postal official. "I have a letter for you from Minot North Dakota."

That got my attention. A letter from Wendy? I hadn't heard from her since Grand View. I ended up staying on at Grand View for the rest of the summer. Amile, romantic at heart, didn't fire me after he heard I missed my shift because fate had remarkably put Wendy and me together for one last encounter. I never took the chance to hitchhike to North Dakota. Now Wendy was possibly back in my life. Fantastic.

I topped off Dorothy's tank. It only took two gallons. "OK ma'am. That'll be $.70."

She handed me a dollar and said, "Keep the change mister. And oh, here's the letter." She retrieved it from the front seat. "I thought it would be nice for you to read at breaktime."

"Thanks Mom."

She handed me the letter, then gave me a quick wave with one hand as she cranked up the window with the other. She put the Olds in gear, exited the drive with a ding-pause-ding, then floored it for home.

Chapter 43 - The Letter

I held out the letter just long enough to make out the name on the return address. Yes, it was Wendy's. I quickly stowed the letter in my slicker away from the weather. I did not want another water drenched note to decipher like the last one she wrote.

Back in the station, out of the sideways rain, I grabbed a fresh pack of Marlboros for a smoke while I took five to read Wendy's letter. I flipped four bits into the till to cover the cigs, sat down on the pay counter stool, and slit the envelope open with my pocket knife. The envelope contained a card and a picture. I lit up a Marlboro and parked it on the edge of the countertop, then focused my attention on the card.

The cover held a watercolor painting of the Grand View Lodge tree swing where Wendy and I met for the first time. The watercolor was signed with Wendy's initials "W L". The entire setting – the elm tree reaching up to its leafy canopy, the swing hanging down just off a gently shadowed lawn – was said in a simple loveliness with just a few brush strokes.

Inside the card were Wendy's words penned in her neat longhand. She wrote of missing me, how our brief time together touched her so. She hoped I was OK. She wondered what my plans were for college.

I took note of something very pleasant. The card not only carried Wendy's message, but also her perfume. I held the card close to my face, inhaled, and was immediately back on the beach with her in our first embrace, feeling the summer breeze cooling our skin. I inhaled again, wishing for her to be real.

The picture held Wendy, posed for her senior high school yearbook. She was beyond cute in a cream-colored turtleneck sweater, staring back at me with a smile and blue eyes that said, "Be here right now Dave, so I can kiss you." Granted, I took some license with that interpretation, but why not round out a wish with a complete thought?

Wendy had packaged the perfect question – did we have another chance together? It was exciting to think about. But it depended largely on the two of us landing at the same college. Intense stuff. Out of the blue. I felt extremely happy that she wrote to me, yet sad that she and I weren't together at that very moment to make plans.

The Marlboro was almost down to the filter. I took the last puff, stubbed it out, and returned to the oil change. Best that I finish the work since the customer was expecting the car first thing in the morning.

As I topped off the oil, I decided to write back to Wendy that night. I would say my feelings for her. My words would likely fall short. This was big love, more fit for a poet to describe. But I would give it a shot. I would tell her my likely destination for college – the University of Minnesota – to give her a target.

Nine PM arrived. I closed the station for the night and hit the road for home on my ten-speed with Wendy's letter safely tucked away in my jean jacket pocket.

Chapter 44 - Parakeets

I wrote back to Wendy that cold rainy night in October. And she wrote back again enthusiastically. We continued to correspond through the fall season of our senior year. Our desire, our love for each other, rose to towering heights in written word, with all the passion Roget's Thesaurus could afford. Wendy's parents were considering the University of Minnesota for her too, so the next year held a real destination for our lives to intersect once again. We savored the adventures we would have. Being on our own together walking the huge urban campus; hanging out in Dinkytown where Bob Dylan came and went; getting to know quirky poets in West Bank coffee shops; wrapping up in dorm room bedspreads to keep the arctic cold at bay. Our future together held such excitement.

Unfortunately, as high school love goes, the passion Wendy and I had for each other chilled unexpectedly. As winter approached, we each experienced a new person in our lives, closer to home. The need to have and to hold, and hold frequently, fueled by raging hormones, won out over our attempt at long distance romance. The person for me was Jan Wright. She had the best parakeets in the Village. I couldn't say no to her Sadie Hawkins invitation. Wendy's new heartthrob was her art teacher, Mr. Dennis. His tilted beret and the art coursing his veins captured her heart.

Wendy sent the first inkling of our demise in one of the last letters between us. She alluded to the relationship that was developing with her art teacher, "Mr. D" – how he was mentoring her whenever they could find time alone. Well that was admirable, I thought. Coincidently, Jan and I had begun a similar mentoring program, although the art of making out was the major topic on our syllabus.

In our final letters, Wendy and I shared the story of our new found loves. Fate allowed us a balanced parting. Each side of love's scale carried an even measure of love to be and love that was. No undercurrent of hurt existed in our goodbye. We left each other softly, as two friends with a special summer romance between us and college to go.

- - -

Nine months later I began my freshman year at the U of M. I couldn't help looking for Wendy, but she was a needle in a haystack of four thousand other freshman on the Minneapolis campus. If she was there at all, I never had the fortune of bumping into her.

I did see her once though. Freshman year was ending. It was late spring. Almost summer. I was on the early bus heading to the West Bank. As Coffman Union approached, a great elm tree reflected from the building's wall of windows. A rope swing hung down from the elm's leafy canopy. There sat Wendy in soft pastels with her journal resting on her lap. She looked content. Beautiful as a watercolor. I waved and hoped she saw me too, as we vanished from sight.

THE END

Epilogue

Five decades ago I washed my last dish at Grand View Lodge. I have had a very full life since then. Fifty years of memories, happy ones for the most part, reside in my head now and spend their time rattling around my brain looking for the exit.

Thoughts of Grand View Lodge make it out on occasion, usually when I situate myself on the red toilet in the family bathroom down the hall. I smile when I recall the antics I shared with the Grand View gang during those innocent days up north, my first time away from home, cavorting about with reckless abandon, learning of love's possibilities when two people reach for each other in the cool pine-scented air of the Northwoods.

I have found over the years that the best times in life are those you don't know you're having. And so it was, that Grand View summer.

W. L.

ABOUT THE AUTHOR

David Ralph Johnson is a writer and photographer when not working his day job as a project manager. He lives in Star Prairie Wisconsin with his wife Theresa and their old dog Jake.